# The BOX
# and the
# BONE

NICELY — TIFFANY, 14   KATE, 10
CARSON, 7   FIFI (POODLE)

BROCKHURST — BUCKY, 11   MUFFY, 9

GARCIA — RAFE, 17   GABE, 13   CARLOS, 10
SUSIE, 8   LUMP (SAINT BERNARD)

ANDERSON — LOTS OF GRANDKIDS

WONG — EDDY, 10   WEB, 8

GRANT — LAURA, 13
NIJINSKY (COLLIE)

PAPPAS — AURORA, 10   ARI, 8   ATHENA, 4

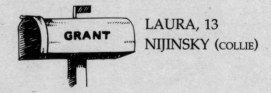

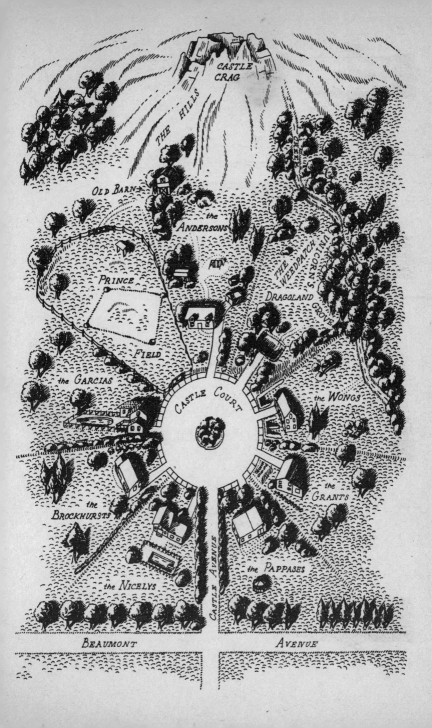

# The BOX
## and the
# BONE

Zilpha Keatley Snyder

A YEARLING BOOK

Published by
Bantam Doubleday Dell Books for Young Readers
a division of
Bantam Doubleday Dell Publishing Group, Inc.
1540 Broadway
New York, New York 10036

The trademarks Yearling® and Dell® are registered in the U.S. Patent and Trademark Office and in other countries.

ISBN: 0-440-40986-1

Printed in the United States of America
July 1995
10 9 8 7 6 5 4 3 2

*To kids and dogs everywhere*

# Chapter

# 1

Carlos Garcia had been digging for a long time. Again and again he tromped on the old rusty shovel, scooped up a bunch of dirt, and threw it as far and hard as he could. He was digging a new private clubhouse in the Dragoland Pit, and the other two PROs, Eddy Wong and Bucky Brockhurst, were digging right there beside him. Sounds like fun, right? *Wrong!* Not so far, anyway.

One reason that digging the new clubhouse wasn't much fun was because the whole thing was just part of a big, fat, humongous argument. An argument that had begun early that morning when Bucky showed up at the baseball diamond carrying a basketball instead of a bat and mitt.

Carlos and Eddy had been sitting on the fence at Prince Field waiting for Bucky for at least half an hour when he finally strolled up the sidewalk. He was wearing his baseball cap on backward and a brand-new pair of Reebok Pumps, and he was carrying a *basketball.* Right away, Carlos had a sneaky feeling that there was going to be trouble. "Look," Bucky said as soon as they'd all said hi, "I'm tired of baseball. How about some basketball? Okay?"

"Oh yeah?" Carlos said. "Basketball today, huh?"

"Sure," Bucky said. "And probably tomorrow too. And the day after that. I'm just plain old ODed on baseball. And besides, it's not baseball season anymore."

Carlos couldn't help smiling a little. He didn't remember Bucky ever paying any attention to what season it was, back when they used to play basketball all year long. But now suddenly it wasn't baseball season anymore—the very next day after Eddy hit his forty-ninth home run. Which meant, according to the rules they'd written up when Mr. A. loaned them Prince Field, that one more home run would make Eddy the first member of the Castle Court *Hall of Fame*.

"Eddy, old Bro," Bucky said in a phony-friendly tone of voice that managed to sound a lot like a threat. "What do *you* want to do today? Huh, dude?"

Eddy didn't say anything right away. Instead he ducked his head so a thick bunch of his straight,

2

black hair slid down to hide his eyes—as well as what he was really thinking. But Carlos could pretty much guess.

Eddy threw his ball into his mitt a couple of times before he answered, and when he finally did he didn't sound particularly happy. "What do I want?" he said finally. "You mean I have a choice?"

"What do you mean, do you have a choice? Sure you do," Bucky said. "We'll vote. Okay?" He looked at Carlos—the narrow-eyed stare that meant "Do it my way—*or else!*" "What's your vote, Garcia? Basketball or baseball?"

Usually Carlos voted Bucky's way, even when he didn't particularly want to. He didn't exactly know why, except that living next door to the greatest fifth-grade athlete that Beaumont School ever had, you just kind of grew up with the habit of being a "team player." That's what Bucky called it—being a team player. But another word for it was *pushover*. And somehow, this time, Carlos wasn't in the push-over mood. However, he wasn't quite able to look Bucky in the eye as he said, "Well, I guess I vote for baseball."

"Yeah?" Bucky said. "You sure, Garcia?" It was a question, but it was also a warning.

Carlos swallowed hard—and said he was sure.

So it was two to one for baseball, and since Castle Court was part of the USA, it was a democracy. Right?

Wrong! Not when one of the voters had it way over the other two in inches and pounds and muscles. And right at the moment Bucky's two extra inches, fifteen or so pounds, and a whole lot of muscle were voting against baseball.

Absolutely against baseball—but after a while the Muscle decided he might not insist on basketball if they could think of something else to do. Something entirely different. And that was how the PROs, as Bucky and Eddy and Carlos sometimes called themselves, wound up digging in the old unfinished basement at Dragoland.

Of course, they'd dug clubhouses there before. Nearly every kid who lived in Castle Court had. The Pit, surrounded as it was by an old brick foundation wall, was a great place for dug-out clubhouses—deep, circular holes with ledges for sitting on all around the edge and a place for a table or fire pit in the center.

When they were only second graders the PROs had cleaned out and deepened an old clubhouse that Carlos's big brothers had started years before. And last year in fourth grade they'd dug a brand-new one. And each time, when the digging was all finished, they'd held a few meetings in it.

The first thing you did at a meeting was to choose a club name and president. (Bucky was always president so that part never took long.) And then you sat around on the ledges talking about other secret stuff. About who would be the club's official enemies, for instance—like a few guys who lived on Beaumont Avenue. And girls, of course. Almost all girls. But the clubs never lasted long. After the fun of digging was over, there never seemed to be a whole lot more to do.

But now they were starting a new clubhouse in a new place. In the farthest corner, where no one had dug before because the ground was too hard and rocky. But Bucky thought the PROs could do it— easy. "It's the best place in the whole Pit for a clubhouse," he said. "Over here in this private corner, all by itself. It's just going to take a little extra muscle, that's all."

So, without saying much more, they'd started digging. There'd been a lot of grunting and puffing as the three of them stomped and scooped and threw, but hardly any talking. No one was saying much of anything. With this clubhouse, even the digging wasn't turning out to be all that much fun.

# Chapter

# 2

Carlos and Eddy and Bucky had been digging silently for about half an hour when Bucky said, "Hey, watch it."

"Watch what?" Carlos asked.

"Where you're digging. This is my place. You're supposed to be over there."

Carlos straightened up and inspected his hands for blisters. "Oh yeah? Why's that?"

"Because I started here, that's why. And Eddy started over there. So this part of the circle"—Bucky walked over and kicked at the ground and grinned one of his "in your face" grins—"this nice solid part is all yours, Garcia."

Bucky went back to digging and after a minute so did Carlos. He slammed his shovel down into the "nice solid" earth and jumped on the top of the blade with both feet. The blade sank into the soil a few inches and then stopped dead with a funny screeching noise. Carlos pulled it out and tried again—and got the same results.

"What was that?" Eddy came over and peered into the hole. "Sounded like you hit something."

Bucky stayed where he was but he obviously was interested too. "Probably just a pipe," he said. "You just hit a pipe."

Carlos put down his shovel and picked up the trowel that was used for finishing the ledges. Crouching down, he scraped away the dirt that the shovel had loosened—and sure enough, right away he began to hit some metal. But it wasn't a pipe. What it was, it gradually became apparent, was *a box*. A box made of some kind of thick metal, like very heavy tin. As Carlos went on scraping and digging around the box, both Eddy and Bucky came over and squatted down beside him.

"It's a chest." Eddy's voice had an excited sound to it. "Like maybe . . ." He stopped and watched for a moment as Carlos's scraping began to uncover a rusty padlock. "Like maybe a treasure chest?"

"Wouldn't be room for a very big treasure," Bucky said.

Carlos went on scraping. "Well, maybe it's papers," he said. "You know, important ones."

"Yeah," Eddy said. "Secret ones. Like about the

Dragomans and why they disappeared. Maybe some papers that would solve the mystery about the Dragomans."

The three PROs stared at each other. Everyone in Castle Court knew about the mystery of the family named Dragoman, who had been the first ones to buy a lot when the Andersons turned part of their farm into a cul-de-sac subdivision. And how, after they'd put in a driveway and a fountain and the foundation for a very large house, they just went away. Some people said it had something to do with a family quarrel, but nobody knew for sure.

But what all the kids at Castle Court did know was that everybody hoped the Dragomans would never come back. Because Dragoland, as everybody called the vacant lot, was such a great place to play.

"Here, let me." Bucky stood up and, shoving Carlos out of the way, began to chop around the edges of the box with his shovel.

Carlos didn't say anything but he didn't move much either. After all, old Brockhurst had just gotten through saying that this part of the circle was his. So whatever was in this part of the circle was his too. Right? So he went on squatting beside the hole and when Bucky's shovel had loosened a little more dirt he reached in and pulled out the box with his own two hands.

It wasn't quite as big as a loaf of bread but it was pretty heavy, and made of metal, all right. Not as thick as iron but heavier than the tin used in tin cans. At each end of the box there were handles that had once moved up and down but now seemed to be rusted into one position. And on the front of the box there was a latch and a small, rusty padlock.

Carlos pulled the box up out of its hole and was beginning to carefully brush off the dirt when Bucky bent over and grabbed it away. Carlos and Eddy, who were both still squatting, stared up at him as he tipped it from side to side and then shook it hard. At the first shake there was no sound at all, but when he shook it again, even harder, they all heard it. A heavy thump and a muffled metallic clatter.

Bucky grinned. "Not papers," he said, "something heavy with lots of pieces. Like gold nuggets, maybe."

"Yes," Eddy said. "Like a bag full of gold nuggets."

"Well, whatever it is it must be pretty valuable or they wouldn't have gone to the trouble of burying it," Carlos said.

The three PROs stared at each other and then at the box. "Well, I'm betting on gold," Bucky said. "Looks like we found ourselves some gold, dudes.

I'll bet it's—" Suddenly he stopped and listened, and right at that moment Carlos heard it too. Somewhere, not far away, someone was yelling Bucky's name.

"Bucky," the voice called. "Bucky. You'd better get home. Right this minute."

Muttering something under his breath, Bucky quickly shoved the box back into the hole and began to kick dirt over it. "It's Muffy," he said. "Look out. Here she comes."

# Chapter

# 3

The mysterious tin box was back in the hole and covered with dirt, and the three PROs had picked up their shovels and were pretending to dig in other places when Bucky's sister, Muffy, appeared on top of the basement wall.

Muffy Brockhurst was nine years old, blond, blue eyed, pug nosed, and very dangerous. Not in the way her brother was, maybe—as in "black your eye and bloody your nose" dangerous. But Carlos knew from experience that, in her own sneaky way, Muffy could be just about as much trouble.

Standing on top of the wall with her hands on her hips she stared down at Carlos and Bucky and Eddy. "You better get home right now, Bucky," she said. "Gary's been waiting for you for a long time and Mom is really mad. You're probably going to get grounded." Gary Harding was a college student who worked part time as a math tutor. Once or twice a week he came to the Brockhursts' for a couple of hours to try to keep Bucky from flunking fifth-grade math. From what Carlos had heard, it was a pretty hopeless cause, but Gary kept trying because Bucky's parents kept paying him.

Still standing on the wall, Muffy tipped her curly blond head from one side to the other and smiled her most dangerous smile. "Another clubhouse, huh?" she said. "Another big, old, super-secret clubhouse." Her tone of voice was definitely sarcastic. Sarcasm was one thing that Muffy had an above-average talent for.

Watching Muffy, Carlos was trying to keep his shoulders from lifting in a nervous sort of twitch, when Bucky whirled around. Grabbing him and Eddy both by the fronts of their shirts, he jerked them toward each other so hard they almost bumped heads.

"Shh," Bucky whispered. "Don't mention the box. And don't touch it till I get back. Okay? Just leave it right where it is until we decide what to do with it. Until all three of us decide, I mean." Then he took off running across the Pit to where Muffy was waiting.

For a while after Bucky and Muffy had disappeared, Carlos and Eddy just went on standing there staring after them. Then, at the very same time, they turned and stared down at where the box was buried. Then Carlos sighed, grinned at Eddy, squatted down beside the hole, and began to brush away the dirt. Began—and then stopped. He looked up at Eddy. "Well, I found it," he said.

Eddy nodded encouragingly. "Yeah, sure. You found it. Go ahead."

When the box was partly uncovered, Carlos wiggled his fingers into the dirt until they were around the handles and pulled up—hard. A moment later the old tin box was sitting right there on the ground between them. Eddy reached out and jiggled the padlock.

"Can you open it?" Carlos asked. "You got any tools with you?"

Eddy, who really liked fixing things, usually carried a bunch of handyman stuff around with him in case something needed fixing. Carlos had seen Eddy fix everything from bicycles to wristwatches with stuff he carried around in his pockets.

Eddy nodded. "I got some stuff, but I don't know if I can open this thing." He reached in his pocket and brought out a small screwdriver and an even smaller pair of pliers.

It wasn't easy. Eddy put the screwdriver into the padlock's keyhole and turned and twisted. And when that didn't work he began to use the pliers too.

"Wish we had the key," Carlos said.

Eddy shrugged. "Probably wouldn't work even if we had it. The whole thing is rusted together. I think we'll just have to pry it apart." Using the pliers to grab hold of the padlock, he began to twist it from side to side, but for quite a while nothing happened. It wasn't until he'd tried three or four times, biting his lip and straining until his knuckles turned white, that there was a grating sound, a click —and the padlock fell apart. The mysterious tin box was open.

# Chapter

# 4

For a moment after the padlock fell apart Carlos and Eddy sat frozen, like they'd been shot by some sort of a paralyzing ray gun. The reasonable part of Carlos's mind was thinking, *I'll bet it's just worthless junk, like rocks or something.* But at the very same time another eager-beaver part was babbling, *Gold! Maybe gold nuggets that have been buried there since the gold rush. Or jewels even. Diamonds and emeralds.*

Then, at the very same moment, he and Eddy both reached out, took hold of the lid, tugged—and it came open with a creaky, rusty squeak.

Carlos noticed the smell immediately. A musty, metallic odor that drifted up from among a bunch of small bags. Small, leathery bags that seemed to be full of something lumpy—and very heavy.

"Nuggets," Carlos whispered.

"Yeah," Eddy breathed.

But it wasn't nuggets—it was coins. Lots and lots of old, discolored, unfamiliar-looking coins. One by one Carlos and Eddy emptied the old, leathery bags out into the lid of the box and examined each bagful one at a time. Some of the coins were nickels and dimes, although the pictures weren't the same as on modern coins. There were larger ones, too, like quarters and half-dollars, and some that weren't familiar looking at all. Nearly all of the coins were covered by a crusty black film. All except the ones in the smallest bag.

There were only three coins in the smallest bag. Large, reddish yellow coins with a woman's head on one side and an eagle on the other.

Carlos was a little disappointed. He really had been expecting diamonds, or at least gold nuggets. He shrugged and grinned at Eddy. "No nuggets," he said.

Eddy was turning one of the yellow-brown coins around in his fingers. "Yeah, but gold, maybe. I think these big ones might be made of gold."

"Oh yeah?"

"Yeah. My dad had a coin collection once. He talks about it sometimes. And he has all these books about coin collecting. I think maybe the gold ones looked sort of like this. I'll take one home with me and see if it's like the ones in the books."

"But we told Bucky we wouldn't take anything. What if . . ."

Eddy nodded and put the coin back into the bag. "Yeah. You're right." He looked around nervously. "And we better get out of here. Somebody else might come along any minute and see this stuff."

Carlos agreed. He'd been feeling a little nervous, too, ever since they'd opened the box. And he went on feeling that way until everything was back the way they'd found it. All the coins back in their bags, the bags back in the box, the broken padlock more or less stuck back together, and the box reburied under a nice smooth layer of dirt.

They were on their way across the cul-de-sac to Prince Field when Carlos asked Eddy if he thought they should tell Bucky about opening the box. Eddy said no right away.

"Yeah," Carlos agreed, "I think so too. You know old Brockhurst. If we told him, he'd be sure to say we took some stuff. You know, to keep for ourselves."

Eddy nodded. "Yes. I think we'd better just pretend we don't know anything. And we'll have to pretend we're really surprised when the padlock breaks as soon as I start trying to open it." He grinned at Carlos. "We'll both be *really surprised*!"

They looked at each other and smiled and then they both did a *big surprise* number.

"Holy cow!" Carlos said. "Would you look at that! It broke."

Eddy made his eyes wide and buggy. "What do you know. Coins! Look at all those crazy old coins!" Then they laughed again, punched each other in the shoulder, and ran the rest of the way back to Prince Field.

# Chapter

# 5

It was an hour or so later, while Eddy and Carlos were still practicing batting and pitching at Prince Field, that Dragoland had another visitor. The new visitor had four feet, a sleek, narrow muzzle, and a beautiful plumed tail. It was Nijinsky, the Grant family's collie dog, and he was carrying an especially large and juicy bone.

And not long after Nijinsky disappeared into the basement pit, still another visitor came down the path. A four-year-old visitor with a curly black ponytail, a polka-dot playsuit on backward, and her shoes on the wrong feet. It was Athena Pappas and she was on her way to play house in the dry fishpond at Dragoland.

Athena was pulling a red wagon and singing in Greek—a song her father always sang while he was working on his sculptures. *"Kato sto yialo,"* Athena sang. *"Kato sto periyiali."*

The wagon was full of all the things a person

would need to play house in a fishpond, like a whisk broom and a piece of chalk, a doll family, and lots of doll-sized dishes and furniture.

Athena parked her wagon beside the edge of the fishpond, took out her doll family, and lined them up so they could watch. She went on singing as she carefully whisked away a lot of dead leaves and outlined all the different rooms with chalk on the nice clean cement. *"Kato sto yialo. Kato sto periyiali,"* she sang over and over again as she worked.

When all the rooms were carefully drawn in chalk she was ready to unload the furniture. It was going to be a very beautiful house with everything in the right place.

She arranged all the beds in the bedrooms first. There were three beds. One real Barbie doll bed made of beautiful pink plastic and two other home-made shoe-box ones. In the bathroom she put an oval-shaped asparagus bowl. Athena hated asparagus but she liked the bowl a lot. It was just the right size and shape for a bathtub. And because she'd gotten a whole kitchen set for her last birthday, the kitchen was best of all, with a sink and stove and refrigerator all made of pink plastic.

After all the furniture was in place and her collection of tiny plastic vegetables and fruit was stored away inside the refrigerator, the house was ready for the doll family to move in. Except for one thing. She'd almost forgotten about her new tea set.

Athena took a last little box out of the wagon, the one that held the new tea set, and looked around the fishpond house. That was when she realized she had a problem. The tea set needed to be on a table and she'd forgotten to bring one. She had remembered to bring a nice white linen napkin for a tablecloth—but nothing at all that would make a good table. For a moment she thought about going all the way back home to find something she could use for a table—but then she remembered something important.

What she remembered was bricks. She was sure she remembered seeing some loose bricks down in the Dragoland Pit. And a nice big brick would do just fine for a table for her fishpond dollhouse.

Athena had climbed partway down to the floor of the Pit before she began to hear a strange noise. A scratching, scraping noise. It sounded like someone was there already, digging a hole. Boys, probably. The people who dug in the Pit were usually boys. Athena frowned. Boys, particularly some of the ones who lived at Castle Court, were creeps. But when she got to the bottom of the stairs and looked around, her frown turned into a happy laugh. It was only Jinsky.

"Jinsky," she squealed. Athena loved animals—all animals. And Jinsky was one of her favorites. Jinsky liked her too. Even though he was busy digging, he stopped long enough to look back over his shoulder and wag his beautiful tail. Then, as Athena ran toward him across the floor of the Pit, he went back to the serious business of burying a bone.

Athena was fascinated. She'd never seen Jinsky bury a bone before. He was digging with both front feet and making the dirt fly out between his hind legs. Being careful to step over the great big bone where it was waiting beside the hole, she moved carefully around the shower of dirt and squatted down to watch. She hadn't been watching for long when Jinsky's toenails began to make a different sound. Like fingernails on a blackboard, only worse. And that was when Athena found the perfect table for her doll family's house.

Jinsky didn't seem to mind. In fact, he seemed quite pleased when Athena pulled the dirty old box out of the hole. With the box gone there was a whole lot more room to bury his bone.

Athena climbed back out of the Pit—carefully because the new table was pretty heavy. She would have opened it up and dumped out whatever was making it so hard to carry, but she couldn't because it was shut with a padlock. Athena knew about padlocks. Her brother, Ari, had one on his bicycle chain.

So she trudged slowly and carefully out of the Pit and all the way back to the fishpond. When she got there the heaviness didn't matter anymore, and neither did the rusty, dirty ugliness. As soon as she'd brushed off some of the dirt and covered the old box with the clean white napkin, it looked just fine. Then she arranged the tea set carefully on top of the new table and the doll family sat down to have a nice tea party.

# Chapter

# 6

All that morning while Carlos and Eddy practiced batting and then went swimming in the Garcias' pool, Carlos kept thinking about the coins in the tin box. He talked about it, too, to Eddy, while they were lying in the sun beside the pool waiting for Bucky to get through being tutored.

"They must be really valuable coins," Eddy said, "or, like you said, why would somebody go to the trouble to bury them?" Suddenly he sat up and began to put on his shoes. "I'm going to go home and look for those books. You know, the ones my dad has about coin collecting. Maybe we can find out how valuable they are."

Eddy took off running and Carlos went on lying in the sun. He must have dozed off for a while because the next thing he knew, Eddy was back, shaking him and saying, "Hey, Carlos. Wake up. Wait till you hear what I found out."

Carlos sat up groggily and tried to get Eddy's face in focus. When he did he realized that Eddy was looking very excited. "Guess what?" Eddy was saying. "You know those yellowish coins? I found a picture of them in my father's books. I think they're called half eagles. And some of them are worth as much as . . . Guess how much."

"I don't know," Carlos yawned. "Maybe—a hundred dollars?"

Eddy grinned triumphantly. "More. A lot more. The book said that if they're in good condition they can be worth as much as four thousand dollars."

Carlos quit yawning *immediately*. "Wow! Really? Four thousand dollars?"

"Yeah, and there are three of them. And some of the other coins might be pretty valuable too. It depends on what condition they're in and what year they are. I wish I'd looked at them more carefully. I wish—" Suddenly Eddy stopped talking and looked at his watch. "Hey. Bucky should be here by now." He put his finger to his lips. "Remember. Don't say anything about opening the box. Or coins. Don't even mention the word *coin*."

Carlos clapped his hand across his mouth. "Not a word," he mumbled. "Punch me if I mention even one coin." Then he lifted a couple of fingers and whispered, "Penny!" and Eddy pretended to punch him in the nose. They both collapsed laughing, but then Eddy looked at his watch and jumped up.

"It's been more than two hours," he said. He got up and ran around to the front of the house and came back looking worried. "The car's gone," he said. "The tutor's car is gone."

It was just a few minutes later, while they were still trying to decide whether to go over and knock on the Brockhursts' door, when Susie, Carlos's little sister, came out on the back deck and yelled at them. "Hey, Bucky's on the phone. He says he has to talk to you guys right away." Carlos and Eddy jumped up and dashed up the stairs and across the kitchen to the phone.

"Look, Garcia," Bucky said as soon as Carlos said hi. "I'm grounded for the rest of the day. So I guess we'll just have to wait until tomorrow. You know, to find out what's in the box."

"Tomorrow!" Carlos said. "Not till tomorrow?" He was really disappointed. So disappointed he forgot to remind Bucky to be careful what he said because there were other phones in the Garcia house and people had been known to listen in. People like his little sister, Susie, for instance. Instead he only rolled his eyes at Eddy and said, "Bucky's grounded. So I guess we can't—you know, open the treasure chest until tomorrow."

Eddy looked really frustrated. "That's not fair," he whispered. "Here, let me talk to him." So Eddy picked up the phone and said, "Look, Brockhurst. Don't *you* want to know what's in it? How about if Carlos and I go dig it up and open it and then we can call up and tell you all about it. I mean, we won't take anything out. You know that."

Carlos couldn't hear exactly what Bucky's answer was, but whatever it was, it was long—and loud. A long, loud, angry roar. Eddy's eyes squinted up and he held the phone away from his ear. Finally he covered the receiver with his hand and said, "Rats. I guess we'd better wait."

"Wait a minute," Carlos said, "let me talk to him again." But when he put the phone to his ear Bucky was still roaring. Something about how digging had been his idea—all his—so that made the treasure his. *All* his, if he wanted to be fussy about it. So they better not touch it till he got there.

Carlos let Bucky go on for a minute before he started to yell back. "Listen, Brockhurst. Just listen a minute. I want to ask you something." And when Bucky finally shut up, Carlos said, "Okay. Okay. We'll wait for you, but does it have to be clear till

27

tomorrow? I mean, you usually don't stay grounded that long."

It was true. Bucky was always getting grounded and usually he found some way to sneak out of the house anyway.

For a minute Bucky just went on breathing hard, but when he finally cooled off enough to start thinking, he said, "Yeah. Well, okay. I'll see. Maybe after dinner when everyone starts watching television. Maybe I can sneak out then. If I can, I'll throw rocks at your windows, like always. Okay?"

So it was all arranged. That evening Carlos would wait in his room, and Bucky would sneak out and throw pebbles at his window and then do the same thing at Eddy's. And then they'd all meet in front of Eddy's garage.

# Chapter

# 7

Susie Garcia knew that listening in on other people's telephone conversations was a bad thing to do. Bad and impolite and something you probably ought to mention the next time you went to confession. But the thing was—sometimes you just couldn't help it. Like when your brother's crummy friend Bucky, who was always doing terrible things, called up and said he had to talk to your brother *right away, right this minute,* because it was something *very important.* At a time like that, it seemed to Susie, it was practically your duty to listen in. So she did.

She listened to what Bucky had to say about being grounded and to what Carlos said about a box that he sometimes called a treasure chest. She also listened to what Eddy said about digging it up to see what was in it—and what Bucky said about how nobody better touch it until he got ungrounded, *or else.* And then, how Carlos and Eddy

29

had finally agreed not to touch the treasure chest until Bucky got ungrounded. In fact, they'd absolutely promised they wouldn't.

So when Susie hung up the phone she knew she had only the rest of that day to find the treasure, dig it up, and hide it somewhere else. She didn't see anything wrong with that. After all, *she* hadn't promised anyone that she wouldn't touch it. And besides, in all the stories hidden treasures always seemed to belong to whoever got there first.

So she would start looking for the treasure right away. Just as soon as she found someone to help her, because looking for treasure all by yourself didn't sound like a whole lot of fun.

That was when she realized that finding a helper might not be all that easy. The problem was—first of all—that the helper had to be a girl. Susie, who had lived for eight whole years, her whole life, in fact, with three older brothers, never had anything to do with boys if she could help it.

Her first choice would, of course, have been Kate Nicely and Aurora Pappas. Kate and Aurora, who were just a couple of years older than Susie, sometimes let her do things with them. Exciting things like looking for ghosts and unicorns, or planning a big, scary war to save some very important trees.

Even though finding a tin box wasn't quite as

exciting as finding a unicorn, Susie had a feeling that Kate and Aurora might be interested. What they'd particularly like about it would be the chance to get the best of Bucky and Eddy and Carlos again. At least Kate certainly would.

But Susie happened to know that Kate and Aurora were away for the whole weekend. The Nicelys had gone to spend the weekend in the mountains and they'd taken Aurora with them. So that left only one other possibility. The only other girl in the whole cul-de-sac anywhere near Susie's age was Muffy Brockhurst. Muffy was a possibility —but just barely.

After Eddy went home and Carlos went up to his room, Susie went out onto the back deck to think. She sat down in the lounge swing and pushed herself back and forth, looking at the Brockhursts' house and thinking about whether to ask Muffy to help her find the PROs' treasure chest.

There was at least one good reason to ask Muffy, and one even better one not to. The one reason Muffy might be a big help was because stealing the treasure would be putting one over on her brother. And putting one over on Bucky was what Muffy liked to do better than anything else in the whole world.

On the other hand, the reason why asking Muffy

might not be a good idea was that Muffy Brockhurst just happened to be the meanest girl in the whole world.

Susie was still sitting in the porch swing, thinking about whether to ask Muffy to help her, when a really interesting coincidence happened. Right at that very moment Muffy came out in her backyard and yelled "Hi, Susie" in a friendly tone of voice.

"Hi," Susie called back—cautiously. That's how you did anything with Muffy—cautiously. Because after you'd known her for a while you found out that when Muffy was being nice there was always a good reason. Sometimes the reason was that she wanted to swim in the Garcias' pool. Or else it might be that she thought you knew something she wanted to find out about.

After Susie said hi back, Muffy climbed over the fence and walked up to the Garcias' back deck. Throwing herself down in a deck chair, she stared at her fingernails for several minutes. Some of her nails were bright red and some weren't. "Want to paint my fingernails for me?" she said finally. "I can't do my right hand."

Susie thought about saying plain old *no*, but then she changed her mind and said, "Not right now, I guess. There's something else that I have to do. Something very important."

"Oh yeah? What? Maybe I'll do it too."

It seemed like a sign. A mysterious sign that she ought to ask Muffy to help find the treasure. Susie's friend Aurora was always getting mysterious feelings about things she ought or ought not to do. So Susie took a deep breath and started telling Muffy all about what she had heard on the telephone. How there was a box, a treasure chest, maybe, that was buried somewhere and how Carlos and Eddy and Bucky were going to go dig it up tomorrow. Or maybe tonight, if Bucky could get himself ungrounded. Just as Susie expected, Muffy was very interested.

"But where do you suppose it is?" Muffy said as soon as Susie had finished. "I mean, didn't they drop any hints about where it was?"

Susie thought for a moment and shook her head. "No. No hints. Except that it was buried."

"Buried! Hey, wait a minute," Muffy said. "They were digging in the Pit today. I saw them when I went to get Bucky to come to his math lesson. I thought they were just digging another one of those dumb clubhouses. But maybe not! I'll bet that's where the treasure is."

Susie jumped to her feet. "Hey! I bet so too. Let's go look."

# Chapter

# 8

A few minutes later Muffy and Susie were on their way across the cul-de-sac. Muffy was still asking questions like, "You sure they didn't say anything about what kind of a treasure it is?"

Susie shook her head. "They didn't say exactly. They just said it was in a box, only sometimes they called it a treasure chest. And Bucky yelled a lot of stuff about how the other guys better not touch any of it until—" She stopped then and said, "Look. There's Athena. Over there in the fishpond." She started to wave but Muffy grabbed her arm and pulled her back behind some bushes.

"Shhh," Muffy said. "We don't want her to see us. She might tell. You know, like if we take the treasure, those jerks might ask Athena if she saw anyone hanging around the Pit. And she'd probably blab about seeing us go in there. Let's go in the back way."

Susie saw what she meant and, for the moment,

at least, she was really glad that she'd asked Muffy to help. When you're doing something as sneaky as stealing somebody else's treasure, Muffy was exactly the kind of help you needed. So they went the long way around and climbed down the back stairs where Athena couldn't see them. Once inside the Pit, Muffy led the way to where she'd seen the PROs digging.

"See, it's got to be right here," Muffy said. "This is where they were when I came to call Bucky. Right here, where there's all this loose dirt. Where's a shovel? There are always lots of rusty old shovels lying around down here."

It wasn't long before Susie and Muffy were both shoveling away like crazy. The dirt was loose and the digging went quickly until suddenly Susie's shovel hit something hard.

"Hey," she said, "I hit something. I think I found the treasure."

She threw down the shovel, dropped to her knees, and began to dig with her bare hands. Right away Muffy did the same thing. Shoving Susie out of the way she began to scratch and claw frantically, getting dirt all over her hands—even under the bright red fingernails on her left hand. Susie sat back on her heels and watched.

A few seconds later Muffy grabbed hold of something and yanked it up out of the hole. It was something hard, all right. A hard, white, *greasy* object that looked horrible and smelled even worse.

"Ugghh!" Muffy threw the gruesome thing down and wiped her hands on her shirt. "What is it?" she squealed. "What is that stinking thing?"

Susie moved closer. "A bone, I think," she said. "A great big bone." She sniffed. "Yep. A great big rotten bone."

"Ugghh," Muffy squealed again, and wiped her hands on Susie's shirt. "I'm going home and wash my hands. Come on. You better wash yours too."

She started off, muttering something about how Carlos and Eddy must have put it there because they guessed that she might come back to see what they were doing. So they moved the treasure and buried that disgusting bone in its place just for meanness. And was she ever going to get even with them. *Was she ever!*

"They did it," she told Susie. "It must have been Eddy and your stupid brother who put that bone in there."

Susie nodded. It must have been her stupid brother. It was just like him. It would have been even more like Muffy's stupid brother, but since he was grounded at the time it must have been Carlos.

. They were already halfway out of the Pit before

either of them remembered about Athena in the fishpond—and by then it was too late. Just as Muffy grabbed Susie's arm and whispered, "Hey. Watch out for Athena," someone said, "Hi. Hi, Susie and Muffy. Whatcha doing?"

It was Athena, of course. Muffy shrugged and turned loose of Susie's arm. Athena was walking toward them carrying a doll in each hand. "Hi," she said again. "I didn't know you were in the Pit."

Muffy stopped and stared at Athena. Then she marched toward her. "Look here, kid," she said, "did you see anybody going into the Pit recently? Somebody like Carlos Garcia? Or Eddy Wong?"

Athena shook her head. "Nope," she said. "No *body*. I didn't see any people body go in there."

"Oh yeah," Muffy laughed. "No people body, huh?" She put her hands on her hips and stared at Athena with one side of her lip curled up. "What kind of English is that?" The tone of her voice, not to mention the look on her face, was definitely sarcastic. "Hey. I'll bet it's Greek. You speaking Greek, kid?" She turned to Susie. "Come on. Let's go." As they started off down the path she went on talking. "Well, somebody put that disgusting bone in there. Ugghh! That bone was really gross."

They'd reached the sidewalk by then and Susie turned around to wave good-bye to Athena before she said, "Yeah, it sure was. So what are we going to do about it?"

"I don't know . . . ," Muffy started to say, but then she stopped, puckering up her mouth and narrowing her eyes. "We'll follow them, that's what, and find out what they did with it. Didn't you say they were going to meet in front of Eddy's garage? You know, after dinner, if Bucky gets out of being grounded."

"Yes," Susie said uncertainly. "They said if. They said they'd meet *if* Bucky could sneak out."

Muffy made a snorting noise. "He'll get out," she said. "He always does."

"Well," Susie said, "I don't know if I can get out."

Muffy gave her a disgusted look. "Sure you can. All you have to do is watch for Carlos to leave, and as soon as he does you come over to my backyard. Okay? If those jerks can sneak out, so can we. Right?"

Susie clenched her fists and stuck out her chin. "Right!" she said.

Back at the fishpond Athena was still standing with the two dolls in her hands, watching as Muffy and Susie disappeared across the cul-de-sac. When they were out of sight she made the doll in her right hand bounce up and down and say to the doll in her left hand, "She said *bone*. Muffy said *bone*."

Then the doll in her left hand said, "Yes. Jinsky's bone, I bet. Let's go see if they took Jinsky's bone."

Athena put down the dolls and headed for the Pit. By the time she'd finished putting Jinsky's nice big bone back where it belonged she was starting to get hungry. So she went back to the fishpond, packed up her doll family, and went on home.

# Chapter

# 9

It just so happened that Rafe was in charge that night at the Garcias'. Carlos's seventeen-year-old brother, Rafe, was usually in charge when both their parents were working late at their restaurant. That was fine with the other kids, because Rafe usually was too busy with his own stuff to be much of a nuisance. And on that particular night it simply meant that sneaking out would be especially easy.

Right after dinner Carlos went to his room and waited for the signal that would mean that Bucky had escaped from being grounded. While he waited he sat by the window and thought about the tin box and the old coins that might be worth thousands of dollars.

At first he was thinking only of what you could buy with that kind of money. Like a new bike and blade skates and all kinds of top-of-the-line sports equipment. He pictured himself walking into a Sporting World store and strolling up to the clerk

40

and going, "Well, let's see. Give me one of these, and two of those and a couple of those over there." It was a fun thing to imagine—for a while. But too much of that kind of imagining can get you into trouble.

Like, for instance, you could start wondering who had owned those old coins in the first place and what *they* had been planning to do with them someday. It was an uncomfortable thought. And it led to an even more uncomfortable one. Like wondering how much of a sin it would be to go ahead and keep all that money—without even trying to find out who the coins really belonged to.

Carlos got up and walked around the room looking for something else to put his mind on. He picked up books and magazines, looked at them without really seeing them, and put them back down. He thought about listening to his Walkman —and realized that he couldn't because it might make him miss Bucky's signal. Time seemed to be going very slowly.

The sun had been down for quite a while before a pebble finally bounced off his window. And by the time he'd tiptoed down the hall, snuck out the back door, and met Eddy in front of the Wongs' garage, it was nearly dark.

"Where's Bucky?" he asked.

Eddy grinned. "Officially?" he asked. Or unofficially?"

Carlos grinned too. "Both, I guess."

"Well, officially he's not here. And we haven't seen him." Eddy lowered his voice to a whisper and tipped his head toward the overgrown hedge that bordered the edge of Dragoland. "Unofficially, he's hiding in the hedge."

Carlos's smile widened. "Well, I guess we better go find him, then. Unofficially, of course."

They didn't have to look very hard. They'd barely turned off the sidewalk into Dragoland when all of a sudden Bucky was walking behind them. Grabbing them both by the backs of their jackets he said, "Okay, you dudes. Let's go. Let's go get that treasure chest."

Under the bushy, untrimmed trees and shrubbery of Dragoland, evening had suddenly turned into night. Deep dark night. Long shadows were everywhere and shapeless blobs of darkness lurked under bushes and oozed out from beneath low-limbed trees. The three PROs walked quickly and quietly—and close together.

At the top of the basement wall they stopped and peered down into the Pit—a bottomless well of darkness. Carlos felt a shiver crawl up the back of his neck. Clearing his throat, he said in what he hoped was a casual, offhand kind of voice, "Hey, it's pretty dark down there. Isn't it?"

No one answered for a second, and then Bucky said, "Dark, smarck. Who cares?" But then he stepped back out of the way. "After you, Garcia. You can go first."

"That's okay," Carlos said quickly. "You go right ahead."

Nobody went anywhere. It was beginning to be a little bit embarrassing when suddenly Eddy came to the rescue.

"Hey," he said. "I'm going to go home and get a flashlight. There's a big one on our back porch."

"Hey, great!" Bucky said. "Just hurry. And if you meet anybody, remember—I'm not here. And you haven't seen me. Okay?"

Eddy said okay and ran, and since his house was right next door to Dragoland he was back in just a couple of minutes. Then, with an extra-large flashlight leading the way, the three of them made their way carefully down the stairs that led into the Pit. After locating a couple of shovels, they moved toward the far corner. To the corner where they'd started their new clubhouse—and where they'd found the tin box.

As soon as they reached the spot, Bucky handed one of the shovels to Carlos. "Here," he said. "You dig."

"What about you?" Carlos asked.

"I'm standing guard," Bucky said.

So while Bucky leaned on his shovel and "stood guard," and Eddy held the flashlight, Carlos did the digging. It didn't take long. After only a minute the shovel hit something with a whack. He dropped to his knees and began to dig with both hands. So did Bucky.

"Oh boy," Bucky said as he pawed at the dirt. "I can't wait to see what's inside this baby. Can you? I can't wait till—Hey! What's this?"

"What's what?" Eddy said, shining the light on what Bucky was holding. And that's when they all saw it. What Bucky was holding up was a very large, very dirty, very disgusting—bone. They stared at the bone and then they all looked at each other in amazement, surprise—and *suspicion.*

"How did that get in there?" Eddy said.

"Yeah." Bucky's voice was tight and accusing. "That's what I'd like to know. How did it?" He threw the bone down and grabbed the flashlight away from Eddy. Shining the light first in Eddy's face and then in Carlos's, he said, "*So* you dudes.

Who do you suppose was fooling around over here while I was stuck at home?''

Carlos and Eddy shook their heads hard. ''Not me,'' they said one at a time. ''Not me.'' And then both together, like an unmusical chorus, ''Not us, Bucky.''

''Oh yeah,'' Bucky said. ''Well, let's see what else you didn't do, then.'' Giving the flashlight back to Eddy he began to dig some more. Carlos did too. Harder and more frantically, as it began to look as if nothing more was buried anywhere in the half-dug clubhouse's hole. Nothing at all.

At last Bucky threw down his shovel and said, ''Okay, what's the gag? Where did you put it?''

''What gag?'' Eddy said. ''We told you. We didn't do anything with it. We left it right here and went off to Prince Field and then we went swimming. Didn't we, Carlos?''

Carlos nodded. ''Yeah, that's all we . . . ,'' he started to say but then suddenly he had an idea. ''Hey, look,'' he said. ''Look at the bone.'' He bent over and picked it up. ''Look at it.''

''I'm looking,'' Bucky said. ''What am I supposed to see?''

''It's greasy,'' Carlos said. ''See here? And there are still some chunks of fat on it.'' He sniffed. ''And it still smells like rotten pot roast, or something. Who do you think would bury a bone like that?"

"Hey, yeah," Eddy said. "A dog. Maybe a dog left it there." Which was exactly what Carlos was leading up to. Eddy was good at that sort of thing. Sometimes he guessed what Carlos was leading up to before Carlos knew himself. "Yeah," Eddy went on. "I mean, who buries bones, anyway? Dogs do."

"Sure," Bucky said. "And then the dog carried off that heavy old tin box in his teeth. Sure he did, Wong. You'd better think of a better story than that."

Carlos had to admit it didn't seem too likely. The box had been too big and heavy—for most dogs. Not your ordinary normal-sized dog, anyway. "Well, I bet Lump could carry that box," he said. Lump, who was the Garcias' enormous Saint Bernard, had a mouth as big as a garbage can.

Bucky's eyes narrowed. "Are you telling me that's what happened?" he asked. "Oh, I get it. Lump carried the box home to your house and—"

"No, no," Carlos said quickly. "I never said Lump did it. Lump is fenced in. He never gets outside of our yard except on a leash. And even if he did, he's way too lazy. I never said he took it. I just said he *could* have."

Bucky glared at Carlos, and for a long time no

46

one said anything. No words anyway. But Carlos could hear Bucky breathing hard. It wasn't a good sign. He tried desperately to think of what might have happened to the box. Of who might have taken it. Because someone did—and he knew that he and Eddy hadn't. But nothing new came to mind and Bucky was breathing harder all the time.

Just then Eddy said, "What I think is we must be looking in the wrong place. You know. Because of the dark. What I think is we better come back and look again tomorrow."

"Yes," Carlos said eagerly, "I'll bet you're right. Let's come back tomorrow and look some more."

"No way." Bucky grabbed the flashlight back and shone it in both of their faces. "We're going to stay right here until you guys come up with that box, if it takes all night. Nobody's going anywhere until—"

Just at that moment a sudden noise wiped out what Bucky was saying. Somewhere in the darkness at the back of the Pit there was a heavy crash, followed by a trickle of smaller sounds. Scratching, spattering sounds, and then a strange animal noise, halfway between a growl and cough. A deep silence followed.

"What was that?" Bucky said in a strangely high-pitched voice.

"I don't know," Eddy whispered. "But it came from back there. Like maybe a wild animal was trying to climb over the wall. Maybe something wild that came down off the hill."

Suddenly Carlos began to get the feeling that, this time, he was the one who knew what Eddy was leading up to. And why. "Yeah," he said. "A mountain lion, probably. Mr. A. told me there were mountain lions around here." The rest of what Mr. A. had said was that there were mountain lions around here *a long time ago*, but it didn't seem like a good time to go into that.

It worked. The thought of a mountain lion seemed to make Bucky change his mind about staying in the Pit all night. Or even for a few more minutes. It wasn't until after they'd dashed across the Pit floor, scrambled over the wall, and ran down the Dragoland driveway that Bucky slid to a stop and panted, "Okay. We'll come back and look again tomorrow. And we better find that box. We just better—or else. You dudes know what I mean."

Carlos thought he knew.

# Chapter

# 10

Susie had never snuck out after dinner before, but it turned out that Muffy was right about it being easy. At least the sneaking-out part was. It was particularly easy that night because both her parents had gone to their restaurant and left Rafe in charge. When Rafe was in charge he always told everybody to go to their rooms and do homework, and then he spent the rest of the evening talking to his girlfriends on the telephone.

That night Gabe and Carlos went to their rooms right away. On other nights Susie would go to her room too—after a while. After she went to her folks' room first and listened in on their telephone while Rafe talked to his girlfriends.

She knew what Gabe did in his room because she could hear him playing his guitar. She wasn't sure what Carlos usually did in his room, but on this particular night she knew exactly what he would be doing. He'd be listening for Bucky to throw a pebble against his window.

So all Susie had to do was go straight to her own room, which was right next to Carlos's, and open her window so she could hear Bucky's pebble too. Of course that meant she had to miss out on hearing Rafe and his girlfriends, but that didn't matter too much. She'd listened to them so many times it was getting to be pretty boring, anyway.

It was a long wait. Susie had read through one short book and was halfway through another before she heard the click of a pebble on glass, and then the sound of Carlos's voice whispering. "Okay. Okay. I'm coming. I'll be there in a minute."

Susie grabbed her jacket, opened her door a crack, and listened while Carlos came out of his room and headed downstairs. Leaning over the stair railing she waited until she heard the back door open and then close softly before she went down too. As she tiptoed down the back hall she could hear Rafe's voice coming from the family room.

"Hey, gorgeous, wait a minute. Just wait one little minute, babe. You know I'd never say anything like that about you . . ." Susie went on tiptoeing.

Out on the back deck she peered over the rail and

down into the Brockhursts' yard. Muffy had said she'd be waiting there, but as far as Susie could tell the yard was empty. It was almost too dark to tell for sure. Susie went on down the steps and started across the yard. She was about to climb over the fence when there was a snuffling noise behind her and something cold and wet touched the back of her neck. It was Lump's nose. Susie stopped to scratch behind his ears. She was still scratching and talking softly, telling Lump what a good dog he was, when a whispery voice said, "Susie? Is that you?" and Muffy's face, witchy pale in the twilight, appeared over the top of the fence. "Is that you?" she said again. "Come on. Let's go. Bucky left a long time ago. Stop petting that stupid dog and let's go."

Susie glared at Muffy. Maybe Lump wasn't the smartest dog in the world, but she didn't allow people to call him stupid. Not right to his face, anyway. She thought about telling Muffy off and going home, but that would mean giving up on the treasure chest, so she just bit her tongue and climbed over the fence. And as it turned out, when they got to Dragoland Muffy suddenly seemed to change her mind about how stupid Lump was.

They were standing on the sidewalk peering into

the dark shadows that lurked under the sighing trees and shivering bushes of Dragoland. "It's dark," Muffy said. "It's really dark in there."

Susie didn't argue. But when she started forward, Muffy pulled her back.

"Look," she said, "why don't you go back and get Lump?"

Susie was really surprised. "Lump? Why?"

"Well." Muffy sounded a little embarrassed. "Dogs can see in the dark better than people. We can kind of let him lead the way. Besides, in case we meet a murderer or something, he can protect us."

Susie couldn't help smiling. The truth was, Lump loved everybody. Probably even murderers and burglars. Susie's dad always said that the only way Lump might catch a burglar was by drowning him in sloppy kisses. But even if he wouldn't be much protection, she wouldn't mind having him along. And she knew Lump would love it.

A few minutes later, when Susie and Muffy were making their way through the underbrush toward the back wall of the Pit, Lump was leading the way. As he pushed under the low-hanging branches and through the jungly vines and bushes, Susie and Muffy clung to his leash and trailed along behind him.

He was quiet, too, for Lump, as if he knew that he shouldn't bark or snort or wheeze the way he usually did. Susie was beginning to think that Lump really was smarter than most people thought he was. That is, until they got to the rear entrance to the Pit.

They were almost to the wall when suddenly Lump's head went up. He sniffed the air loudly and began to make a happy whining noise.

"Shh!" Muffy whispered. "Shhh! Make him hush up, Susie."

"It's Carlos," Susie whispered back. "I think he smells Carlos." She took her hands off the leash to grab Lump's muzzle but at that very minute he lunged at the wall and tried to jump over.

Fortunately Lump was too fat and floppy to be much of a wall jumper. He didn't quite make it over, but he did manage to drape his front half over the wall for a minute and knock loose a few bricks. As the bricks tumbled down noisily inside the Pit, Lump fell back down outside. And then, when Susie jerked on his collar, he began to make a terrible noise, choking and coughing and moaning like some kind of a half-strangled monster.

Pulling frantically on the leash, Susie and Muffy finally managed to get Lump away from the wall and back into the shadows. They crouched there for several seconds, waiting for the sound of footsteps and the sight of angry faces appearing above the wall.

But nothing happened. Nobody came. After a minute or two Susie tied Lump to a tree limb and crept quietly back to the wall. She got there just in time to see a bobbing flashlight beam and three running figures. The three figures dashed madly across the floor of the Pit, scrambled over the wall, and disappeared into the night.

When Susie got back to where Muffy and Lump were waiting, Muffy said, "Didn't they hear it? Didn't they hear the noise your stupid dog made?"

Susie giggled. "Yes, they heard it, all right. It scared them to death. When I peeked over the wall they were running like scared rabbits."

"Really?" Muffy giggled too.

They both went on giggling for a while before Susie said, "I don't think they found what they were looking for. They weren't carrying anything."

"Good," Muffy said.

"So, what next?" Susie asked. "What are we going to do now?"

Muffy shook her head. "I don't know. I guess

we'll just have to go on following them till we find out where the treasure is. You can follow Carlos and I'll follow Bucky, and when they're with Eddy, we'll both follow all three of them."

That sounded all right to Susie.

# Chapter

# 11

When Athena woke up the next morning it was Sunday already. She knew what day it was because she could hear the bells ringing way down at Susie's church on Beaumont Avenue. She was glad it was Sunday because that meant Aurora was going to be home very soon.

Climbing out of the old crib that had been Aurora's and then Ari's before it was hers, Athena went to the window and looked out. The sky was gray instead of blue, and there wasn't any sunshine. She shivered and headed for her closet to get something to wear. Something warm because of no sunshine.

But all the warm things were hanging high up and Aurora wasn't there to reach up and get them down. And nobody else was up yet. Except for Aurora, nobody at the Pappases' got up very early. Athena's mother and father, who were always called Diane and Nick, were too tired from painting and sculpturing, and Ari was just too lazy.

Putting on the same playsuit she'd worn the day before, the one with the front and back that were hard to tell apart, Athena skipped down the hall. When she got to the kitchen she pushed a chair in front of the refrigerator, climbed up, and got out three slices of frozen Sara Lee French toast. Then she jumped down, put the French toast on the seat of the chair, and pushed it over to the microwave. She climbed up again (without stepping on the toast—at least not very much), put the toast in the microwave, and very carefully pushed the right buttons. Then she got down and got out the syrup and butter while she waited for the microwave to say *ping, ping, ping,* which meant it was all finished cooking.

It didn't take long at all because she'd been making her own French-toast breakfasts since she was three years old. She was just climbing up onto her own chair to start eating when her brother, Ari, came into the room.

Ari's curly hair was flat on one side and his eyes looked fat and sleepy. He sniffed the air, looked at Athena's breakfast, and went to the cupboard for a plate. Then he sat down at the table and looked at

Athena's breakfast some more. After a while he said, "You don't want *all* that French toast, do you?"

Athena pulled her plate closer. "Yes, I do," she mumbled around a mouthful of toast and syrup. Ari went on staring at Athena's plate for a few seconds before he sighed and got up and went to the refrigerator. By the time his breakfast was ready his eyes had opened wider and he was starting to talk. Ari always talked a lot, except when he was sleepy. Today, the first thing he talked about was when Aurora would be coming home.

"Sometime tonight," he said. "The Nicelys' said they'd start home in the afternoon and probably stop someplace for dinner. So they won't be here until pretty late."

Athena was disappointed. Aurora had said Sunday and Athena had been thinking Sunday morning, maybe. She was so disappointed her lower lip began to feel wobbly, but she wasn't going to cry. Athena didn't like crybabies. Instead she swallowed hard and said, "Then can I play with you today? Can I play with you, Ari?"

Ari grinned. "Sure. I'm going to work on my newspaper today. I'm going to write newspaper stories. You want to write a newspaper story too?"

Ari was teasing. He knew she couldn't write many words yet. She could read a whole lot of words and write her own name too—which Aurora said was very good for four years old—but she couldn't write a story yet and Ari knew it. She glared at him, climbed down out of her chair, and ran down the hall.

Only a minute or two later she was on her way down the back steps pulling her red wagon. Since there wasn't anything else to do and nobody to play with, she was going back to Dragoland to play in the fishpond. But halfway down the back steps the wagon tipped over and spilled everything out.

"Oh rats!" Athena said, which was what Ari always said when things went wrong. She stared at the mess where everything had fallen out of the wagon onto the sidewalk. Then she said some Greek words that she wasn't supposed to say but that her father said when he was angry. She went on saying the words angrily while she pulled the wagon back right side up and started putting everything back in. She had already been angry—at Aurora for being gone so long and at Ari for teasing her. And now she was angry at the wagon for dumping everything out.

After she'd said the Greek words two or three

times she started talking to the wagon. "You stupid wagon," she said. "Look what you did. You broke everything all to pieces, I bet."

But everything wasn't broken. Not really. When Athena picked up the dolls and their furniture the only "broken to pieces" things she found were one teacup and the padlock on the old box. The padlock was broken all to pieces, the box lid had come open, and lots of little red bags had fallen out.

The bags that fell out of the box looked just like one that belonged to Athena's grandma. Her grandma's bag was very old and it was full of jacks that she'd had since she was a little girl. When Athena was at her grandma's house she played with her grandma's jacks. She wasn't very good at it yet but she was getting better.

But when Athena opened the bags she was disappointed. There weren't any jacks or anything else you could play with. Just some dirty old pennies and nickels.

She said "rats" again and dumped all the bags back in the box and wrapped it up again in the napkin. Then she started off up the sidewalk pulling the wagon behind her.

She was almost past the Grants' when Jinsky trotted out from behind the house and lay down on the lawn. Athena went over to say hello. She petted

Jinsky and hugged him and shook his paw—Jinsky always liked to shake hands—before she went back to her wagon and went on to Dragoland.

But seeing Jinsky had made her remember about how Susie and Muffy had dug up his nice big bone and had thrown it away. And how she, Athena, had had to put it back where Jinsky wanted to keep it. And because she was already angry at Aurora and Ari and the wagon she felt angry again at Susie and Muffy. Angrier than ever. When she got to the fishpond she decided she'd better go see what other mean things Susie and Muffy had done.

So, after carefully parking the wagon by the fishpond she went on down the path and climbed up over the wall and into the Pit. And, sure enough, when she got there she found that Jinsky's bone had been dug up all over again. She was starting to put it back in the hole where it belonged, when she suddenly changed her mind.

There wasn't any use burying the bone in the same place again and again. Not if Susie and Muffy were going to keep digging it up.

"I'll just take it back to him," Athena said. "I'll put Jinsky's bone in my wagon and take it to his house and tell him to bury it someplace else."

Back at the fishpond she put the bone in the wagon along with all her dolls and furniture and started off to look for Jinsky. Sure enough he was still there lying on the grass in his yard with his chin on his front paws. When Athena put the bone down in front of him he sniffed at it and wagged his beautiful tail. Athena knew that was Jinsky's way of smiling, so she smiled at him, too, and told him he'd better find a new place to bury his bone. Then she went back to her wagon.

She was almost to Dragoland when she turned around and went home instead because she needed to go to the bathroom.

# Chapter

# 12

That morning Carlos decided to go to early mass with his mother for a change. That way he'd be free later to go to Eddy's before Bucky was up and around. So he got up very early, jumped into his clothes, and rushed downstairs—and a minute later Susie came downstairs too.

"Well, look who's up," he said. "What are you doing up so early?"

"I just felt like it," Susie said. "What are you doing up so early?"

"I'm going to early mass today with Mom."

"Oh," Susie said. "I am too. I'm going to early mass too."

Carlos thought that was a little strange because both he and Susie usually went to eleven o'clock mass with their dad. But it wasn't until they were back at home again that Carlos began to notice something even stranger. What he noticed was Susie going upstairs every time he did, and coming back down when he did, and sitting right beside him while he ate breakfast. But it wasn't until he went out on the deck to feed Lump and she was right there, too, that he began to get really suspicious.

"Hey, kid," he said as Lump was inhaling his second can of Science Diet, "are you following me, or what?"

Susie whirled around from where she was leaning over the deck railing, looking startled—and a little bit guilty. "Following? Following you? No. Of course not. Why should I want to follow you?"

Carlos said he didn't know why, and he didn't, but just the same he was careful, a little later, when he was getting ready to go to Eddy's house. He was careful not to slam the door to his room, he tiptoed down the hall, and he even went out the back way because the front door tended to squeak. He didn't think Susie followed him that time. At least he didn't catch her in the act.

Eddy had been up for quite a while when Carlos got there—the Wongs were really early risers—so Carlos didn't even have to wait for him to finish breakfast. In fact he didn't have to wait at all. He'd no more than gotten inside the door when Eddy grabbed him and dragged him down the hall to his room.

"I've been reading the coin books some more," he whispered as soon as he'd closed the door. "And *wow!* Wait till you see what I found out." Rushing across the room he plopped himself down on the floor and pulled two large, flat books out from under his bed. "Come on, sit down here. Wait till you see this!"

Eddy had marked a couple of pages in each book with strips of paper, and now he began to open them to the markers. "See here," he said, "see this picture. That's a gold coin that's called a half eagle. Don't you think that looks pretty much like the ones in the bag? You know, those three coins that were in the bag all by themselves."

"Yes," Carlos said uncertainly. "They looked something like that. I remember that they had a bird like that on one side. And a woman's head on the other."

"That's what I remember too. And they were the same brassy color, instead of blackish brown like the other coins."

"And so," Carlos said, "if they *are* half eagles they're real valuable, huh?"

Eddy pointed to the page. "Just read that," he said. "Right there. Right there where it says six thousand dollars. Some of the rare ones are worth as much as six thousand dollars."

"I thought you said four thousand."

"Well, that was before I finished reading. See, the thing is, a lot of it depends on other stuff. Like on special little markings that mean they were part of a certain minting. Like, see this one in the picture that has a little letter *D* right here near the bottom. Sometimes a letter like that makes them a lot more valuable. And other things make a difference too. Like what year they were minted and how worn out they are."

Eddy sighed and hit the page in frustration. "I just wish I'd looked at those coins more carefully. You know, when we opened the box."

Carlos wished he had too. But he'd been kind of nervous at the time, thinking that Bucky might come back and find out that they'd broken the padlock and looked in the box. And besides, he'd had no idea then that they were so valuable. "Well, we'll just have to find them so we can look at them again," he said.

"Yeah, you're right." Eddy looked at his watch. "Hey, look what time it is. Bucky should be up by now. We'd better get over there."

Eddy shoved the coin books back under his bed and was starting for the door when Carlos pulled him to a stop.

"Uh—wait a minute, Eddy," he said. "I've been

thinking about . . . I mean, somebody hid those coins. So maybe they still belong to that person. You know, like legally and all?"

Eddy nodded slowly, biting his lower lip. "Yeah, I did think about that," he said finally. "But what I decided was—that box was buried a long, long time ago. And if the person who put it there were still alive he'd have been back by now to dig it up. What I decided was that the person who buried it must be dead by now. Don't you think so?"

While Carlos was still deciding what to say, Eddy began to grin. "Besides," he said, "I can just see us telling Bucky that we have to start looking for the real owner. I mean, can't you guess what old Brockhurst would say to that?"

What Eddy said was true, all right, and it made Carlos feel a little better. And then he said something that was even truer. "Anyway, there's no use wasting time worrying about it right now. There'll be plenty of time to worry about stuff like that after we find it again. Right?"

Carlos sighed with relief. "Right," he said.

They were partway down the hall when Eddy said, "Remember, don't say anything to Bucky about coins."

"Oh yeah, no coins. Just gold nuggets. Bucky is sure it's gold nuggets."

"Yeah, big fat nuggets," Eddy said, and they marched down the hall whispering, "Nuggets, nuggets, nuggets!"

Eddy stopped in the kitchen long enough to ask his mom if it was all right for him to go to Bucky's with Carlos, and then they took off running. They were just starting across the cul-de-sac when Carlos grabbed Eddy, pulled him to a stop, and pointed back toward the Grants' front yard. Nijinsky, the Grants' collie dog, was lying on the front lawn gnawing on a bone. A great big, dirty, stinking, very familiar-looking bone.

# Chapter
# 13

Back at her own house, Athena parked the wagon in the driveway and went in the back door. It was nice and warm in the kitchen. Ari was still eating his breakfast, and Diane, their mother, was at the stove making herself a poached egg. Diane was dressed for work already, in her painting clothing— a green sweater with blue and purple painty spots, and blue jeans smeared with orange and yellow. When she saw Athena she picked her up and hugged her. Snuggling her face against Athena's cheek she danced around the kitchen singing, "How's my beautiful baby?" over and over again in English, and some other things in Greek.

Ari made a snorting noise. "Beautiful?" he said. "She looks like a mess to me. Her playsuit is dirty, not to mention on backwards, and her ponytail's all crooked."

Diane pushed Athena away and looked at her. Then she took the rubber band off Athena's ponytail, smoothed it down with both hands, and put the band back on. Cocking her head to one side she said, "There. That's better." Then she ran her hands down Athena's arms and said, "You feel cold, baby. Here, wear this. This is nice and warm."

Diane took off her painty green sweater, put it on Athena, buttoned it all the way down the front, and rolled up the sleeves into big fat doughnuts around Athena's wrists. Then she kissed her three more times and went back to her poached egg. Athena ran down the hall to the bathroom.

When Athena got back to where her wagon was waiting in the front yard she was feeling better. Diane's sweater was painty and it had raggedy elbows but it was nice and warm—and long. So long it went down almost to her feet. Feeling nice and warm made Athena forget about being angry at Aurora and Ari, and the wagon, and Muffy and Susie. She began to sing her favorite song again as she went across the lawn.

"*Kato sto yialo. Kato sto periyiali,*" she sang as the wagon bounced behind her across the bumpy lawn. When she got to the sidewalk she stopped to think.

Yesterday, she'd played all the things she could think of about the fishpond house. Today it might be more fun to find someplace new. Someplace where she could make an even better house for her doll family. Maybe there would be a better place at Beaumont Park. Turning the other way she started down the sidewalk toward the avenue. The park would be a good place to play.

But Athena had gone down Beaumont Avenue for only two blocks when it started to rain. Just a few big fat drops at first, but then more and more. She was almost to the big church where Susie's family went every Sunday, when the rain began to come down very hard and fast. People were coming out of the church, putting up umbrellas, and hurrying to their cars. Athena stopped under a tree and watched until the people were gone.

The rain was coming down harder and harder all the time. Big drops were coming right through the tree and falling on Athena and her wagon and the doll family too. She began to run. With the wagon banging along behind her she ran up the sloping ramp that led to the porch in front of the church door.

It was better under the little roof. Pulling the wagon up next to the church's big double doors, Athena picked up the doll family one by one and dried them off on the sleeve of Diane's sweater. Then she leaned against the door and waited for the rain to stop.

But it didn't stop, and after a while the wind began to blow so hard that the rain started coming right in under the little roof. Athena was leaning back further to get away from the rain when suddenly the door began to move—and when she pushed harder it moved some more. Pulling her wagon behind her, she went on in.

Inside the big church doors there was a room with tables and pictures around the walls, and some other doors that led to an even bigger room with a very high ceiling. Leaving the wagon in the first room, Athena went on in to look around. It was very beautiful inside the church. She looked at all the benches for sitting on and at all the statues and pictures and candles. Then she went back to the smaller room to wait for the rain to stop.

While she was waiting Athena looked at the pictures and notices on the walls and tried to read what they said. She could read words like *you* and *call* and *school* and *children*.

The word *children* was on a box that sat up on short wooden legs near the front door. There was a picture of children on the box too. Lots of skinny little children with sad eyes and thin, hungry faces. Athena looked at the picture of the sad, sick children for a long time, and at the box behind it.

The box was like a bank for saving money, with a narrow hole in the top to put the money in and with one wall made of glass so that you could see how much money was inside. The money was all mixed up together so it was hard to tell, but it didn't seem like there was very much. Not enough to buy food for all the skinny little children in the picture. Looking at the little bit of money made her feel sad.

After a while Athena remembered that she had some money too. She had two pennies in her playsuit pocket. She pulled up Diane's sweater, reached into her pocket, and dropped the two pennies into the hole on the top of the box. It was fun dropping the pennies into the hole. And afterwards, when she looked at the pictures of the hungry children and then at her own two pennies lying there in the box with the other money, she didn't feel quite so sad.

Athena had to wait in the church for a long time. Every now and then she went to the church door to see if the rain had stopped. After a long time it almost did. The sidewalks were still wet and the sky was gray and cloudy, but not much rain was coming down. She closed the door quickly and went back inside to get her wagon and the doll family.

The family had been waiting very patiently. Athena picked up the mother doll and the little girl doll and made them sit down beside each other. "Look," she made the mother doll say, "look baby. The rain is stopping. We better go home right now."

"Oh no," the girl doll said. "I don't want to go home yet. I want to stay here in the church. Let's go see all the statues and candles. And the money for hungry children. I want to see the money box for hungry children."

Athena played with the girl doll for a little while longer before she finally pulled her red wagon out through the church's doors. The rain was all gone, the sun was shining, and she was feeling especially happy.

# Chapter

# 14

When Carlos and Eddy saw Nijinsky with the bone, they forgot, for the moment, about hurrying over to Bucky's. Instead they went back and squatted down on each side of Nijinsky to do a more careful inspection. Just to be sure the bone was the same one that they'd found the night before, buried where the treasure chest had been.

Carlos and Eddy leaned closer. With some dogs it might be dangerous to get so close in a bone-chewing situation, but with Nijinsky you didn't have to worry. He only wagged his tail and stopped chewing long enough to let them have a good look.

"Yep," Carlos said. "It's definitely the same shape, and see all that gunk stuck to it? I remember all that gunk."

Eddy wrinkled his nose and made a gagging noise. "And the smell too. I definitely remember the smell."

"Well, I guess Nijinsky was the one who dug up

the treasure. You know, when he was burying the bone."

"It looks that way," Eddy said. "At least we know that he must have been the one to put his bone there."

Carlos sighed and nodded. "Well, anyway, I guess we better go tell Bucky."

"Yes. I guess so," Eddy said.

As they started back across the cul-de-sac Carlos asked, "What do you think he'll do to Nijinsky when he finds out?"

Eddy grinned. "Oh, he'll give him the third degree." He got a mean look on his face and said, "Okay, dog. You better start talking—or else."

"Yeah," Carlos said. "Or else—the torture chamber. Bring out the red-hot pokers, Igor. And the thumbscrews."

Eddy did an Igor the hunchback number and whined, "Too bad, Boss. No can do thumbscrews. No thumbs."

They were still laughing when they rang the Brockhursts' bell and Bucky shot out the door.

"Okay, dudes," he said, "let's go. I'm ungrounded. Let's go find that treasure. Let's go dig up . . ."

Carlos had been saying "er, er, er" for quite a

76

while before Bucky shut up long enough for them to tell him about Nijinsky and the bone.

As soon as they'd convinced him that it was, for sure, the very same bone, Bucky said. "Well, all right. That means . . . Well, I guess that means that . . ."

"Well, for one thing it means that Nijinsky has been back to the Pit since we were there last night," Carlos said.

"That's right," Eddy agreed. "But that's about all it means for sure. It doesn't prove that he had anything to do with—"

"What do you mean?" Bucky said. "Sure he did. His bone was in the hole, wasn't it? And our treasure chest was missing from that same hole. That sounds like a pretty good clue to me. Come on. Let's go look. Maybe he buried the treasure somewhere else in the Pit."

Carlos didn't think that was too likely. That would have to mean that Nijinsky dug up the treasure and carried it away and buried it someplace else. And *then* came back and buried his bone in the first hole. Not too likely. Nijinsky seemed like a fairly smart dog, as dogs go, but not all that smart. But there was no use arguing with Bucky so the three of them headed back to the Pit.

On the way Bucky wanted to stop at the Grants' to see the bone but Nijinsky had disappeared. And so had the bone. So they went on to the Pit and started digging.

The first place they dug was in the corner where they'd started the new clubhouse and found the tin box. "Just in case we missed the right spot in the dark last night," Bucky said. "Everybody dig where you were digging before. And don't stop until you're down to the really solid stuff."

In Carlos's part of the circle that didn't take long. But he was still whacking away at the "solid stuff" when he heard something and looked up in time to see a huge, shaggy shape come flying over the Pit wall, dragging something behind it. The shaggy shape was Lump and the something he was dragging at the end of his leash turned out to be Susie.

As Susie landed on her hands and knees she turned loose of the leash and Lump came bounding toward Carlos whining with happiness. Carlos braced himself for a slobbery kiss attack. Then as soon as he'd gotten Lump to more or less cool it, he went to see if Susie was hurt. She was still sitting on the ground looking at her knee, but when Carlos came over she jumped up.

"You all right?" he asked her.

"I'm okay. I'm okay," Susie said, even though

she obviously had a skinned knee. "Hey, I didn't know you guys were in here. I was just taking Lump for a walk."

Carlos grinned. "Down here in the Pit? Funny place to walk a dog, isn't it?"

"No, it isn't. It's a great place to walk a dog. You can just walk around and around down here. See, like this." She grabbed Lump's leash and began to limp around the Pit. Carlos went back to where the other two PROs were watching, leaning on their shovels. The three of them went on leaning on their shovels while Susie walked around the Pit a couple of times, limping a little and acting very strange. Then she and Lump climbed back out and disappeared.

"Weird," Bucky said. "Okay, you dudes. Get back to work."

A little later the PROs gave up on the clubhouse area and began to move out around the whole Pit looking for places where the earth had recently been disturbed. Carlos was beginning to dig in a new spot when Eddy came over and stood next to him.

"Don't look now," he said. "But over there, to your right, in that bushy place. Somebody is hiding in those bushes and looking over the wall. With binoculars. I'm sure I saw some binoculars."

"Oh yeah?" Carlos said. He checked on Bucky to see if he had noticed, too, but he seemed to be busy digging. "I'll check it out," he told Eddy. But by the time he'd eased over to the wall the bush was empty. The binoculars, and whoever had been looking through them, had disappeared.

Carlos went back to digging, wondering if the person in the tree had been Susie again. Except—as far as he knew—Susie didn't have any binoculars. And if it wasn't Susie, who was it? The whole thing was beginning to give him a slightly creepy feeling.

# Chapter

# 15

"That's a bad scrape," Brigitta Garcia, Susie's mother, said as she unwrapped a large-size Band-Aid. "How did it happen this time?"

"It was Lump's fault," Susie said. "He pulled me down. He just happened to see Carlos and he took off like a rocket and jerked me off my feet."

"Well, perhaps you ought to let the boys walk Lump from now on," her mother said.

"But I like walking him. Dad lets me do it."

Her mother finished packing up the first-aid kit before she said, "Well, I'll talk to your father about it. But it seems to me that walking a dog who weighs more than you do is not a good idea."

Susie limped out onto the back deck and collapsed in a chair to wait for her knee to stop hurting. Actually, it had been Muffy's idea, and it hadn't been a good one. Pretending to be walking Lump in the Pit so she could check on what the PROs were doing would have been dumb even if she hadn't fallen down and skinned her knee. Because those creeps obviously weren't going to be doing anything important while she was there. The whole thing had been stupid.

She hoped Muffy had had better luck. Peeking over the wall with your mother's opera glasses made a little more sense than trying to pretend you were just an innocent dog walker—instead of a spy. She sighed. As soon as her knee felt better she would have to go back to the Pit—but without Lump this time—and go on following the PROs.

While Susie was collapsed on the back deck waiting for her knee to quit hurting, the three PROs were still going over every inch of the Pit floor, searching and digging. Carlos was just about to suggest, for the third or fourth time, that they give up and do something else, when Bucky suddenly yelled, "Look. I told you so. There he is."

Sure enough, there he was. The four-legged suspect, Nijinsky, was standing at the Pit entrance—*and* he was carrying the same big bone. But when Bucky yelled he turned around and disappeared.

Bucky threw down his shovel and started toward the stairs. Halfway there he stopped and looked back. "Come on, you goons. Get a move on. We have to follow him."

*Why?* Carlos was thinking. *Why do we have to follow him?* And when they caught up with Bucky, Eddy asked more or less the same question. "What do we want to follow Nijinsky for?" he asked. "You think he has the box on him, or something? Like in his pocket, maybe?"

Bucky gave Eddy a cold stare. "Can't you figure anything out? He obviously came here to bury the bone again. Right? And he left because we were here. So now he's probably going to bury it someplace else. *Like*"—he made his face say, "Now listen carefully, you retards," as he went on—"like in one of his other burying places. Like, for instance, in the place where he buried something else just last night."

Carlos didn't know if Bucky could be right—but then again, he supposed he could be. He looked at Eddy and shrugged and the two of them followed Bucky across the Pit and up the stairs. They got to the sidewalk just in time to see Nijinsky turning into the Andersons' driveway.

"There he goes," Bucky yelled. "Come on. Get a move on."

Two little Anderson grandkids came out to watch as Carlos trotted through their front yard. He felt stupid running across their lawn following Eddy, who was following Bucky, who was following a dog with a big, stinky bone in its mouth. He didn't blame the Anderson kids for looking bewildered.

The kids were still staring wide eyed as the whole procession turned to the right and ran right on through the Andersons' property, along the Prince Field fence, and on out through a grove of trees. They had passed the Andersons' old deserted barn and were starting up the hill toward Castle Crag when Eddy caught up with Bucky and tried to talk to him.

"Look, Brockhurst," he panted, "I don't think . . . Why are we? . . . I mean, what's the point of? . . ." But Bucky, and a few yards ahead Nijinsky, just kept on jogging. So Carlos and Eddy kept on going too.

A little way past the big old jagged boulder known as Castle Crag, Nijinsky suddenly stopped and sat down. Dropping the bone, he licked his chops and turned to look back over his shoulder. And then he grinned. Carlos was almost sure of it.

But when Carlos started to walk up to where he was sitting, Bucky held him back. "Shh," he said. "Maybe this is it. Maybe he's going to start digging."

"This is *what?*" Eddy asked.

"This is where he buries things. When he doesn't

bury them in the Pit." Bucky made a sarcastically patient expression like "I'm making this as clear as I can," and said slowly, "Don't you get it? This is probably where he buried the box."

But then Nijinsky quit grinning, picked up his bone, and went on running. They were quite a way past Castle Crag when it started to rain.

"Hey," Carlos said, "it's raining. We'd better head for home."

"Forget it," Bucky said. "A little sprinkle won't hurt you. That's all it will be this time of year. Just a little sprinkle."

A few minutes later the rain was coming down in bucketfuls, the wind was howling, and the three PROs were squeezed back against the trunk of a pine tree, soaking wet, cold, and miserable.

Nijinsky had disappeared. They hadn't seen him go. He'd been there right in front of them just a minute before, but then, while their eyes were full of rain, he suddenly was gone. They huddled under the tree and shivered for a long time while the rain seeped down through the branches and dripped off their ears and the tips of their noses.

Nobody talked for quite a while, but at one point Carlos said, "I wonder where Nijinsky got to?"

"Huh," Bucky said. "He's probably somewhere around here digging right this minute. Dogs aren't afraid of a little rain. If you guys weren't such dweebs we could be out there watching him dig up the treasure."

Carlos wiped the rain off his face and said, "Feel free, Brockhurst. Go right ahead."

"Sure," Bucky whined, "and have you guys sneak off on me while I'm gone."

So nobody went anywhere. The three PROs waited under the tree, getting soggier and soggier, for a long time.

# Chapter

# 16

After the rain stopped, the sky got blue again. The sun began to shine and went on shining until it turned red and went down behind the hills. Athena sat on the Pappases' front steps and watched the sky and sun. She was really waiting for the Nicelys and Aurora to get home, but they didn't, so she watched the sun go down instead. But when it began to get dark and cold she went indoors and sat in her favorite place under the piano and practiced writing her name in the dictionary.

Nick and Diane were still working in their studio and Ari was busy working on his journal. Athena couldn't find any paper to practice on so she was writing in the big dictionary. She had decided to write her name on every single page, and she was already on page twenty-three when Aurora came home.

After they'd hugged each other Aurora told her all about the beautiful mountains and lakes and chipmunks she'd seen at the Nicelys' cabin, and then she helped Athena go to bed. But it was hard to go to sleep because there was so much to think about. Athena thought about Aurora being back home and about the beautiful chipmunks. And then she thought about how hard it had rained that day and all the things she had seen and done while she was waiting in the church. It was a long time before she went to sleep.

But when she woke up the next morning everything was back to normal. Aurora and Ari had breakfast cereal and went to school, and Athena had French toast. And then she went back to play at Dragoland. She was on her way there, pulling her doll family in the wagon when she found Laura Grant's ballet slippers.

Laura Grant, who lived next door to the Pappases, was one of Athena's favorite people—even though she was a teenager. Aurora and her friend Kate Nicely hated teenagers. At least Kate said they did.

So Athena hated teenagers too. At least most of them. All except the ones who were ballet dancers and who belonged to a nice dog like Jinsky. And who were thin and beautiful with lots of long dark hair and a soft friendly smile. Athena especially liked the friendly smile. Kate said that some people at Castle Court thought that Laura Grant was unfriendly. Aurora said that was only because she was shy.

But Laura Grant wasn't ever shy or unfriendly to Athena, so when Athena found the ballet slippers in the wet grass she wanted to do something to help.

The slippers were near the sidewalk, where Laura must have dropped them when she was on her way to school that morning. Maybe while she'd been running to catch the bus.

Athena looked up at the sky. It was gray and rainy looking again, and she was sure that being rained on wouldn't be good for ballet slippers. She sat down on the sidewalk and looked at the slippers and wondered what to do. She knew it wouldn't help to knock on the Grants' door, because both of Laura's parents went away to work every day.

While she was still wondering Jinsky came around from behind the house. When he saw Athena he bounced over to say hello and while Athena was patting him and shaking his paw he noticed the slippers too. At first he only sniffed them and wagged his tail, but then he picked them up in his mouth and trotted off. When he got to the Grants' front porch he lay down and began to chew. Just in time, Athena dashed up the steps and grabbed the slippers away.

She was still standing on the Grants' front porch when suddenly she knew just what to do. She went back to her wagon, unwrapped the old tin box, and opened the lid. Sure enough, just like she thought, it was the perfect size to hold two pink ballet slippers. She put the slippers inside and closed the lid. Then she put the box right by the sidewalk so Laura would be sure to see it when she came home. She went on to Dragoland then, feeling very good because Laura's ballet slippers were safe and sound. Of course she didn't have a tea table anymore, but that was all right. A nice big brick would be almost as good.

That same Monday morning at recess, when Susie Garcia came out of the third-grade classroom at Beaumont School, Muffy Brockhurst was waiting for her. "Come here," she said. "Hurry. I'm supposed to be playing soccer."

Muffy was telling the truth—for once. Susie could see Muffy's fourth-grade class out on the soccer field. "Why aren't you?" she asked. "Playing soccer, I mean?"

"Because we have to talk," Muffy said. She wrinkled her pug nose. "Besides, I hate soccer." Then she frowned and leaned closer. "Did you follow Carlos yesterday, like I told you to? You know, after they left the Pit and went away somewhere?"

"No," Susie said. "I didn't." She pointed to her bandaged knee. "I skinned my knee really bad when Lump pulled me down in the Pit. I had to go home and get it doctored. And after my mom got it bandaged . . ." She shrugged. "They'd disappeared. I looked in the Pit and everywhere, but they weren't there." She was telling the truth. After her knee quit hurting she'd gone to the Pit, and then she'd called the Wongs and the Brockhursts. And nobody seemed to know where the three guys had gone.

Muffy put her hands on her hips and glared at Susie. "So," she said, wagging her head from side to side, "you hurt your poor little knee and you had to run home to Mommy. And you let those guys get away and they didn't come back for a long time. Not till after it stopped raining. And when they did get back they were all sopping wet and covered with mud. Like maybe they'd been digging somewhere. *Get it! Digging!* And we don't know where because you let them get away."

Susie glared back. "Well, where were you? Why didn't you follow them?"

"Because I was hiding. Carlos must have seen

something when I was peeking over the wall with the binoculars, because all of a sudden he started coming toward me. So I ran down across the Weedpatch and hid by the creek. And by the time I got back they were gone. But I didn't worry too much because I thought you must have followed them."

"Well, I didn't."

"Well, didn't you even ask Carlos where he'd been? Like, when he got back home all sopping wet."

"Sure," Susie said, "I asked him."

"And . . . and . . . what did he say?"

"He just laughed and went, 'How soon do you have to know?' That's what he always says when I ask him something. Did you ask Bucky?"

Muffy shrugged. "Oh sure."

"What did he say?"

"The usual. Like, 'Get lost, dog meat.' And some other stuff your mommy probably wouldn't want you to hear."

Susie glared, because she hated it when Muffy treated her like a little kid just because she was in third grade and Muffy was already in fourth. She started to walk away but Muffy grabbed her arm. "Look," she said, "this was all your idea in the first place. You were the one who found out about the treasure and asked me to help find it."

"I know it. But what can we do now?"

"I don't know. Except we've got to keep following them. Because that way, sooner or later, they're going to lead us to where they put the treasure. And then we can get it away from them. Okay?"

Susie sighed and said okay but she wasn't feeling too hopeful.

# Chapter

# 17

"Just to look around," Bucky was saying as the three PROs got off the bus on Castle Avenue that afternoon after school. "We won't dig or anything. I just want to see what the rain did down there in the Pit. Like, maybe it washed away some dirt and uncovered something we missed. If you know what I mean."

Carlos knew what he meant. But he was hungry and what he really wanted to do was go home and get something to eat. "Well, okay," he said. "But just to look around. No digging."

While they were still on the bus Carlos had noticed Laura Grant. She had been sitting near the front, and when the three PROs started around the cul-de-sac toward Dragoland, there she was again, walking right ahead of them. Carlos was watching her because he was interested in the way she walked, as if her feet hardly touched the ground. He'd thought before that Laura Grant could be a great athlete if she were just into track and field instead of ballet. He was still watching when, right in front of her own house, she stopped and picked something up. As the three of them walked on past, Bucky and Eddy were busy ignoring Laura, like they usually did with girls. But Carlos looked at her and said, "Hi." *And* saw very clearly what she was holding in her hands. A few yards farther on he grabbed Bucky and Eddy and pulled them to a stop.

"Look!" he hissed. "Look at what Grant's got."

"What do you mean, what she's got?" Bucky said.

Eddy peered around Bucky's shoulder. "You mean like measles or zits or something?" he asked.

"No. In her hands. What she's holding. I think it's . . . It looks like our box."

They all stared.

"Hey. You're right," Eddy whispered. "That's our treasure box, all right. See those handles on the ends and all those rusty places. What's she doing with our box?"

"That's what I'm going to find out," Bucky said. "Right this minute." He started back down the sidewalk, and Carlos and Eddy followed.

Laura Grant was still standing in the same place holding the box in both hands. She was turning it this way and that and opening and closing the lid. The padlock seemed to have disappeared. When she looked up and saw the PROs coming she smiled, looked again—and her smile faded. Carlos glanced at Bucky—and saw why. Bucky was doing his Rambo stare. He swaggered up to Laura Grant and said, "Okay, Grant. What are you doing with our box?"

Laura's too-big eyes seemed to get even bigger. "Your box? Is this your box?"

"It sure is," Bucky said. "What's in it? Tell us what's in it, okay. That'll prove that it's ours."

She looked puzzled. "My ballet slippers are in it." She opened the box and held it out for them to look. "See. But I didn't put them in there. They were just there when I picked it up."

Bucky narrowed his eyes. Reaching out, he grabbed the box out of Laura's hand. "Sure they were," he said sarcastically. He took out the ballet slippers and threw them on the ground. "Then what's this? What are these things?"

He held the box out for Laura to see. When Carlos looked, too, his stomach did a funny loop-the-loop, because in the bottom of the box were some old leather bags. Some *empty* old leather bags. Carlos glanced at Eddy. Eddy was making his lips into a "shhh-ing" shape. Carlos knew what he meant.

Eddy meant that nobody had better mention the word *coins*.

"See," Bucky said, picking up one of the bags and shaking it in Laura's face. "What was in these bags? Just tell me that. What was in there when you 'found' our box?"

"I told you," Laura's voice was soft and shaky, like she might be about to cry. "I never saw that box until just a minute ago." At that moment Nijinsky dashed out from behind the Grants' house, ran to Laura, and jumped up to lick her face. Then he bounced around the lawn a few times before he sat down near her feet.

Bucky stared at Nijinsky. Stared—and nodded his head slowly up and down. You could almost see a lightbulb coming on over his head. "I get it," he said. "Now I get it." He started shaking one of the bags in Laura's face again. "That's how you 'found' our box. Isn't it? Your dog brought it to you. Well, he stole it. That mutt of yours dug up our box and stole it, and you'd better cough up everything that—"

Suddenly Bucky quit yelling and looked down at Nijinsky—and at a whole lot of *big white teeth*.

"*Grrr*," Nijinsky said.

Bucky backed slowly away. Laura put her hand on Nijinsky's head. Then in one graceful motion she turned, picked up her slippers, and started down the path to her front door—floated down the path as if her feet hardly touched the ground. Nijinsky trotted along beside her, and nobody went after her or yelled at her to stop. Not even Bucky.

After Laura disappeared inside her house Carlos and Eddy crowded around Bucky and stared at the box. It was the same one, there was no doubt about that. But what happened to all the old? . . . Carlos clamped his lips shut tightly and looked over at Eddy. Eddy nodded.

Then Bucky said, "Come on. Let's go to my house. We can talk there—about what we're going to do to get our treasure back."

Eddy and Carlos said okay and they started across the cul-de-sac. All the way across, Bucky went on raving about what they were going to do. "We've got to work up a plan of attack. About how we're going to get our treasure away from that Grant dude. If that sneaky female thinks she's going to get away with stealing our gold nuggets, she's going to find out . . ."

They were passing the planter area in the middle of the cul-de-sac's circular drive when Carlos heard something. A kind of rustling noise that seemed to be coming from under some big ferns. And out of the corner of his eye he thought he saw something too. But when he looked again it was gone. He could still hear the rustling sound. It sounded too big to be a bird or a squirrel, but Bucky was making so much noise it was hard to be sure.

# Chapter

# 18

When the three PROs disappeared into the Brockhursts' house there were more rustling noises in the planter area. Then a voice whispered, "Ouch. You dumb klutz. You crawled on my hand." The voice was Muffy Brockhurst's.

"I couldn't help it," Susie Garcia whispered back. "They were going to see me. I had to move or they would have."

Muffy crawled out from under a fern. "Ugh," she said. The ground in the planter area was muddy from yesterday's rain, and now Muffy was too. She stood up and wiped her hands on Susie's back. Susie crawled out of reach and stood up too. "They went in your house," she said.

"I know," Muffy said. "Did you hear what they were saying? I heard part of it."

Susie nodded uncertainly. "A little. I heard just a little. Bucky was saying something about making plans. And gold nuggets. I'm sure I heard him say 'our gold nuggets.' "

"Yeah, I heard 'gold nuggets' too. That must be what's in the treasure chest. Come on. Let's go to my house. Maybe we can spy on them some more there."

As they were crossing the drive Susie said, "Did you see them talking to Laura Grant? I wonder why they were talking to her? And then it looked like Nijinsky almost bit Bucky."

"Really," Muffy sounded delighted. She stopped and stared at Susie. "Wow! I wish he had."

"Yeah," Susie said. "It sure looked like it. It's funny though. I didn't think Nijinsky would ever bite anyone."

Muffy made a snorting noise. "Not anyone except my brother, I guess," she said. "Nijinsky's a smart dog."

They'd reached the entryway of the Brockhursts' house by then and Muffy stopped to wipe her feet on the doormat. "Hey, wipe your feet," she said. "My mom will strangle you if you mess up her white rugs."

As Susie wiped her feet she was thinking that Muffy was probably exaggerating again. But knowing the Brockhursts, she wasn't too sure. As soon as she'd wiped her feet very carefully, Muffy opened the door quietly and they went on in.

They went through the downstairs first, peeking into each room before they went in. No one was on the first floor except Muffy's mother, who was in her office talking on the telephone. Muffy's mom, who sold houses and subdivisions, had a little office right next to the kitchen.

"They must have gone up to Bucky's room," Muffy whispered. "Come on. Be very quiet."

Muffy led the way up the stairs then and down the hall. When they were tiptoeing past Bucky's room she stopped for a minute and put her ear against the door. But then she shook her head and led the way to her own room, which was right next to Bucky's. Opening the door she jerked Susie inside.

"Hurry up," she said. "They're in there, in Bucky's room. I could hear their voices but I couldn't tell what they were saying. Wait here a minute. I'll be right back."

Muffy went out and down the hall and a minute later she was back carrying two drinking glasses.

"Here." She handed one to Susie. "Do like this." Muffy went over and put the top of the glass against the wall. Then she put her ear against the bottom of the glass. She motioned to Susie. "Here. Put yours right here. This way you can hear through the wall.

It was an interesting idea. Susie put her glass against the wall and listened—but she couldn't hear very much at all. She kept on trying—pressing her ear to the bottom of the glass harder and harder until it began to ache. Now and then she could hear Bucky yelling something, but most of it wasn't very clear.

In the next room Carlos and Eddy were sitting on Bucky's bed while Bucky paced up and down the room. "She was lying," he yelled. He made his eyes big and round and in a high-pitched, squeaky voice that was supposed to be like Laura's he said, " 'I never saw that box until a minute ago.' Sure she didn't. She probably took our gold nuggets out and buried them someplace as soon as her mutt showed up with the box. Well, we'll show her. Will we ever!"

"What are you—er—what are we going to do?" Carlos asked.

"Well." Bucky swaggered around the room. "We'll just do a little arm twisting. We'll wait for her when she gets off the bus tomorrow and then we'll grab her and—"

"What about Nijinsky?" Carlos said.

For a minute Bucky didn't say anything. But after a while he started up again. "Okay. We'll just follow her. Every time she steps out of her house, or off the bus, we'll be there. Right behind her. Not touching her or anything. Just following along behind her. You know. Staring at her like . . ."

Bucky narrowed his eyes and looked as sinister as he could, which in Bucky's case was pretty sinister. Sticking his hands in his pockets, he slouched around the room looking up out of the tops of his eyes.

Eddy didn't look too impressed. "And what's that supposed to accomplish?" he asked.

"Oh nothing much," Bucky sneered. "Just scare her to death, that's all. Scare her so much that she'll decide it isn't worth it. So she'll give up and hand it over."

Carlos couldn't help grinning. "You mean that you think just because you go around staring at her, that she's going to hand over all those valuable coins? Just like that?"

It wasn't until he caught a glimpse of Eddy's face that he realized what he'd said.

*"Coins?"* Bucky's eyes were really narrow now. "What do you mean—coins?"

Feeling a little bit panicky, Carlos stared at Eddy.

But after a second, Eddy shrugged and grinned. "Hey, it's okay," he said. "I was already thinking that maybe we ought to tell him."

"Tell me what?" Bucky said.

So they did. All about how, on that first day when they'd just found the box, and after Bucky left for his math lesson, the two of them had opened the treasure chest.

"That padlock was old and rusted and it just fell apart," Eddy said.

"And . . . ," Bucky yelled. "And what was in it?"

"Coins." Carlos looked at Eddy and grinned. "You know. Pennies and nickels and dimes. And like that." He waited until Bucky's face fell about three feet before he went on and told the rest of it. All about how old the coins were—and about the three gold coins in the separate bag. Then Eddy took over and told what he'd found out about how the gold coins might be worth six thousand dollars apiece.

"Six thousand," Bucky howled. "Wowee! Six thousand apiece. And the other coins are probably worth something too. That's . . . That's . . . How much is that, Wong?"

"Oh maybe around twenty thousand dollars," Eddy said.

"Wowee! Twenty thou. That's enough to buy a Harley Dyna Glide."

Eddy and Carlos looked at each other and shrugged. There wasn't much point in mentioning that Bucky's part would be only one-third of twenty thousand. Or, for that matter, that it would be seven years before he could ride on a Harley even if he did get one.

Suddenly Bucky stopped daydreaming about motorcycles. Frowning again, he looked up out of the tops of his eyes. "Okay," he said. "So now we start trailing the Grant dude for sure. I mean, we're going to make her think that she's never going to have a minute's peace for the rest of her life. Not until she gives us back our coins—or else twenty thousand dollars." Bucky went to his window and looked out in the direction of the Grants' house. *"Twenty thousand!"* he yelled. "Twenty thousand dollars, or else."

In the next room, Muffy and Susie took their ears off the drinking glasses and looked at each other.

"Did you hear anything?" Muffy asked.

Susie shook her head. "Not much. It was all kind of mumbly. But I'm pretty sure I heard Bucky say, 'twenty thousand dollars.' "

"Holy cow," Muffy said.

# Chapter

# 19

The next afternoon, Athena was just leaving Dragoland when a bus stopped on Castle Avenue and Laura Grant got off. Athena began to run with the wagon bouncing behind her. She liked talking to Laura. She wasn't going to talk about putting the ballet slippers in the tin box, though, because that was a secret. Athena liked having secrets.

But when Laura was just passing Athena's house she stopped suddenly and looked behind her. Athena saw them then too. The three boys who called themselves PROs, Carlos and Eddy and—worst of all—Bucky were walking right behind Laura. As Athena watched, Laura turned around and said something to the boys and they yelled something back. Athena stopped running and started listening. After a while she pushed some dolls and furniture out of the way and sat down in her wagon to watch and listen some more.

At first she couldn't quite hear what Laura was

saying but she did hear something that Bucky Brockhurst said.

"Okay," he was shouting. "If you don't like it you know what you can do."

But then, when Laura was quite a bit closer, Athena began to hear what she was saying too. "Stop it." Laura's voice was tight and shaky, almost like crying. "Just stop following me."

"Sure," Bucky said. "We'll stop. As soon as you give back what belongs to us. Just hand it over and we'll clear out. Won't we, dudes?"

Bucky looked at Eddy and Carlos when he said "dudes" so Athena guessed he meant them. They both nodded their heads, but Athena thought they didn't look too happy. Particularly Carlos. Carlos kept looking away in other directions like he didn't want to look right at Laura while Bucky was yelling at her.

Carlos was looking away in another direction when all of a sudden he yelled, "Hey! Hey. Look over there. Somebody's hiding in the bushes. Just like before. I thought someone was in there yesterday but I wasn't sure. See? Right over there in the planter area."

"Oh yeah," Bucky said. "We'll see about that. Come on, you dudes."

While the three "dudes" started across the cul-de-sac, Laura came on up the sidewalk. When she got to where Athena was sitting in her wagon she stopped to say hello.

"Hi, Athena," she said, smiling her nice friendly smile.

Athena said hi too. She was starting to ask Laura what was the matter and why Bucky was yelling at her, when he started yelling again. But this time Bucky was yelling at somebody he was pulling out from under a bush. The somebody was his sister, Muffy Brockhurst. And Susie Garcia was there too. Carlos and Eddy were pulling her out from under another bush. Then they were all yelling at each other. Standing there in the middle of the road, all five of them were yelling their heads off.

Right at first Athena couldn't tell what any of them was saying, but just then a truck came down Castle Avenue, turned into the circular drive, and honked its horn. So they all came over to the sidewalk—right next to where Athena was sitting in her wagon.

"Okay, what's coming off here?" Bucky was saying. "What do you dweebs think you're doing following us around?"

Muffy stuck her chin up in the air and said, "We can follow anybody we want to. Can't we, Susie? I mean, it's a free country, isn't it?"

"Yeah," Susie said. "And besides, you're following Laura, aren't you? If you guys can follow Laura, why can't we follow you? Why are you guys following Laura?"

Muffy looked at Susie in surprise. In pleased surprise. "Right," she said. "Why are you dudes following Laura?"

"That's none of your business, dog meat," Bucky roared. "And you better keep out of this, if you know what's good for you."

By then they were all around Athena's wagon. Laura and Muffy and Susie were on one side and Bucky and Carlos and Eddy were on the other. Athena sat in her wagon and looked back and forth as they went on yelling. It was all very interesting.

Muffy yelled at Bucky and Susie yelled at Carlos and then everybody yelled at everybody. The yelling went on and on, and Athena went on looking back and forth, until everyone seemed to run out of breath at the same time. Suddenly it got kind of quiet. And then Carlos said something. Not yelling. Just talking.

What Carlos said was, "This is stupid. This whole thing is stupid. I'm outta here." He turned to Bucky. "Brockhurst, I'm through with this whole stupid mess."

# Chapter

# 20

The next few days, Bucky wasn't speaking to Carlos. Not even at school. And that meant that Carlos didn't get to be on the best team anymore, because it was Bucky's team and he got to choose who was on it. Eddy was still speaking to Carlos but only when Bucky wasn't looking.

Once on Wednesday, or perhaps it was Thursday, when Bucky wasn't looking, Carlos asked Eddy what Bucky was planning now. About Laura and the gold coins.

Eddy laughed. "The latest thing is that he's going to sue. He says his dad is always suing people and usually it works really well. He says he's going to get a lawyer to write up a paper. You know, a paper that says to give back all the coins or else she'll get taken to court. He says that's the kind of thing his dad's lawyers write up."

"But I thought lawyers cost a lot of money," Carlos said. "Like hundreds of dollars. Where's Bucky going to get that kind of money?"

"Yeah, I know. His other idea was, it wouldn't be a real lawyer. Just someone who writes real well who could write something that would sound real legal. You know, like a real lawyer did it."

"Like who, for instance?"

"I don't know for sure. He was kind of thinking of Ari Pappas. You know, Ari writes all kinds of stuff." Eddy laughed. "Bucky says Ari would be really cheap. All he'd have to do—" Eddy made his voice deep and scary, "—he'd just have to go, 'Okay, Pappas. Take your choice. You write the paper or your arm gets broken.' "

"Great," Carlos said. "Just great." But at that moment he saw Bucky heading their way. "Well, I'm outta here," he said. "See you later."

That was about how things went for the rest of the week. When Sunday came Carlos went to late mass with his father, as usual. Everything at church was the same as always, too, until right at the end when the priest was making announcements about classes and things like that. Only this time there was another announcement.

This time Father Andrew asked everyone to notice the extra page that was in the bulletin that morning. Carlos hadn't noticed the extra page, and he still wasn't noticing it, until Father Andrew said something that really caught his attention. What he said was something about a "very valuable coin collection." That was when Carlos really started listening.

Father Andrew was talking about the wonderful secret gift that someone had made to the fund for hungry children. Actually the priest said "anonymous" gift but when Carlos poked his father and asked, he found out that "anonymous" meant "secret." Someone had donated the coin collection without letting anyone know who he was. Father Andrew also talked about how the collection had turned out to be very valuable—particularly the *three gold coins*—and how many hungry children it would save from starving. Father Andrew also said that he understood the donor might not want any publicity, but that he deserved great honor and glory, which he would surely get in heaven. Carlos went home from church in a kind of daze.

Right after lunch he called Eddy and asked if he could come over.

"Sure," Eddy said. Then he laughed and said, "Bucky keeps saying that you are dead." He made his voice sound like Bucky's and said, "Garcia is dead, man. I mean *dead*, until he gets smart and starts helping us tail the Grant dude again." Eddy laughed again. "So come on over. I like talking to dead people."

So Carlos went to Eddy's house and as soon as he got there he handed him the page from the church bulletin. Eddy read it over, stared at Carlos, and read it over again. Then he said, "Well, that's it. That's our coin collection for sure."

"That's what I thought," Carlos said.

They both stared at each other for a while longer before Carlos said, "Should we show this to Bucky?"

"Sure." Eddy grinned. "Why not?"

"Well, for one thing, because he might think I did it. I mean, my whole family goes to Saint Patrick's."

"Well, you didn't do it, did you?"

Carlos shook his head slowly from side to side. "Absolutely not. I didn't even know there was a collection box for hungry children until today."

Eddy nodded. "I believe you," he said. "Let's go tell Brockhurst."

They went on talking about it as they walked across to Bucky's house. About who took the box and why they donated all the coins to the hungry-children's fund.

"Wait," Carlos said. "I just thought of something. If we convince Bucky that I didn't do it, he'll probably go on blaming Laura. Even though she doesn't go to our church."

"So what?" Eddy said. "At least he'll know that she can't give it back now, even if she wanted to. So there won't be any reason to go on following her. Right?"

"Right," Carlos said. "That will be one good thing, huh?" He sighed. "But I wish I *knew* who did do it. I mean, who took the box in the first place and why they just gave it away like that. It sure is a mystery."

Just then the little Pappas kid came up the sidewalk pulling her red wagon. She looked up at Carlos and Eddy and said, "Hi, dudes."

Eddy and Carlos both laughed and Carlos said, "Hi dude, yourself, kid." Then they both stepped aside and let Athena pull her wagon between them and on up the sidewalk.

After she'd gone past, Eddy said, "Yeah. It sure *is* a mystery. Do you suppose we'll ever find out who did it?"

Carlos shrugged. "Naw," he said. "I don't suppose so. The funny thing is, all of a sudden it doesn't seem to matter all that much."

Eddy gave him a funny look, but then he began to nod his head. "Yeah," he said. "I guess I kind of feel the same way."

"And another good thing," Carlos said. "Maybe now we can stop digging holes and following people and get back to something important. Like playing ball."

Eddy nodded. "Right on." But then, as he rang the Brockhurst doorbell, he added, "Baseball or basketball?"

"Baseball!" Carlos said. "What else? Everybody for baseball say 'It's a free country.'"

They were both yelling "It's a free country" at the top of their lungs when Bucky Brockhurst opened the door.

**CASTLE COURT KIDS**

Look for the complete adventures of the
Castle Court Kids!

### The Diamond War   0-440-40985-3

The boys want to chop down some trees to build
a baseball diamond. But Kate and her friends are
determined to stop them in this fast-paced summer
adventure.

### The Box and the Bone   0-440-40986-1

Carlos and his pals find a buried treasure, but
before they can cash it in, it disappears. There are
plenty of hilarious mix-ups as they try to figure out
who's got the loot.

### Ghost Invasion   0-440-40987-X

Kate and Aurora are hunting for ghosts on Hal-
loween. When Bucky and his friends find out, they
plan a little haunting of their own. Anything can
happen when the ghosts start rising in this comic
thriller.

### Secret Weapons   0-440-40988-8

Two sinister men are lurking around Castle
Court. Could they be terrorists? With a little help
from their science projects, the kids go after the bad
guys in a hilarious—and smelly—showdown.